"That part you mentioned about me being ready to pounce?"

Aidan's eyes wandered over Brianne with slow deliberation. "You couldn't be more right. I'm guessing you've got about three seconds before I zero in on my next target."

She couldn't have moved to save her life.

Not with his gaze cruising over her with every bit of sensual heat she'd ever longed for ten years ago. More. She would have never guessed back then that a man's stare could ignite a small inferno.

For that matter, she hadn't known until just this red-hot, blistering second. If she'd had any doubt about who Aidan's next target might be, it was obliterated the second he moved toward her. Invaded her personal space. Crowded her.

This was a bad, bad idea. Her hungry lips and aching body didn't seem to realize it, however.

"Does this remind you of anything, Bri?" His voice was close. Too close. He bracketed her body with his arms, steadying himself on the wall behind her.

Did it? If she wasn't careful, she'd be so lost....

Dear Reader,

Ever since I lived in Miami Beach, I've never missed an opportunity to rave about the colorful setting and the vibrant mood of the place. But the challenge remained—how could I possibly convey the nuances of the infectious energy of the nightlife, the lure of Latin music, the draw of Caribbean cuisine and the steady backdrop of rolling waves behind it all?

Lucky me, I've got six books in which to try! Welcome to SINGLE IN SOUTH BEACH, my first miniseries for Harlequin. This month we begin with one of the new owners of the exotic Club Paradise and over the course of the series we'll meet more of the driven women who put their creative muscle behind this hedonistic playground. Next month, be sure to check out Summer's story in Blaze #108, *Girl's Guide to Hunting & Kissing*.

For now, sit back and enjoy Brianne Wolcott and Aidan Maddock's story. Since these two hit the town, nightlife on the strip has definitely heated up! Visit me at www.JoanneRock.com to learn more about my future releases or to let me know what you think of my books.

Happy reading,

Joanne Rock

Books by Joanne Rock

HARLEQUIN BLAZE
26—SILK, LACE & VIDEOTAPE
48—IN HOT PURSUIT
54—WILD AND WILLING
87—WILD AND WICKED

HARLEQUIN TEMPTATION
869—LEARNING CURVES
897—TALL, DARK AND DARING
919—REVEALED

SEX & THE SINGLE GIRL

Joanne Rock

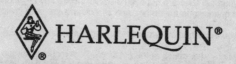

HARLEQUIN®

TORONTO • NEW YORK • LONDON
AMSTERDAM • PARIS • SYDNEY • HAMBURG
STOCKHOLM • ATHENS • TOKYO • MILAN • MADRID
PRAGUE • WARSAW • BUDAPEST • AUCKLAND

For fabulous Lisa, Jen and Arete—
my highly educated, superintelligent girlfriends whose advice
I crave most for shoes, shopping and great food.
Who says we can't still be divas? I adore you.

ISBN 0-373-79108-9

SEX & THE SINGLE GIRL

Copyright © 2003 by Joanne Rock.

This edition published by arrangement with Harlequin Books S.A.

Visit us at www.eHarlequin.com

Printed in U.S.A.

Prologue

"HOLD ON TO YOUR PANTIES, girlfriends. It's raining men just outside our front door." Brianne Wolcott eyed the monitor from security camera number three, the one with the best view of the crowd gathered at Club Paradise's Ocean Drive entrance—and all the gorgeous guys waiting in line. The mob of people would be checking out the newly revamped disco in another hour. Nervous energy hummed through her. As a new part-owner and head of security for the club, Brianne needed to make sure tonight's reopening ran smoothly. "Looks like we're in for a busy night."

"My panties couldn't be more firmly in place if they were Super Glued to my hips." Lainie Reynolds, CEO of the reorganized South Beach resort and nightclub, slid into the oversize leather chair behind Brianne's desk in the slick, modern office housing the club's high-tech equipment. "Divorce will do that to you."

The four founding members of the soon-to-be hottest spot on Miami's trendy South Beach had called a meeting an hour before they opened their doors for business. Although Club Paradise had been a wildly successful resort for couples over the last five years, the three former partners behind that business—known locally as the Rat Pack—had absconded with the profits.

Brianne's stepfather had been one of those partners, Lainie's husband another.

With Lainie's business savvy and legal guidance, the women left behind in the wake of the embezzlement scheme had pulled together to restructure the company. Tonight they were reopening just the club. In a few weeks, they'd have the rest of the resort refurbished and ready for guests.

The couples theme was out, however. Given that three of the four women who now owned the business had been deceived by husbands or boyfriends in the Rat Pack, the new owners had no desire to market themselves for the sticky-sweet couples' demographic. Club Paradise would slowly be overhauled into a singles' haven—a lush, hedonistic oasis for the uninhibited.

And although Brianne hadn't been dumped by a husband or boyfriend in the Rat Pack—merely inconvenienced by her highly immoral stepfather—she'd still bought into the singles theme. She had a hideous track record in the dating world, and even worse experience as part of a couple. She couldn't wait to enjoy the lavish, sensual luxuries the club would provide.

Summer Farnsworth, another founding partner and the ambiance coordinator for the club, approached the television screen teeming with men. She blew a kinky blond curl out of her eyes and traced a finger over a muscle-bound motorcycle rider who had pulled in front of the line outside. "I don't know, Lainie. Even Super Glue might not be strong enough to resist the temptations we are going to be subjecting ourselves to in this line of work. Have you seen these guys?"

Brianne suspected Summer would be the quickest to find romance—or at least some sensual diversion—during the course of their upcoming endeavor. Sort of a flower child throwback, Summer prided herself on lack of inhibitions and what she called "living in the moment." While Brianne had never considered herself uptight, next to earthy Summer and her seductive wardrobe of silk skirts and halter tops, Brianne sometimes feared her tailored clothes and dark colors made her look downright repressed.

"Been there, done that," Lainie shot back, slowly spinning in the oversize black leather chair behind Brianne's seldom-used desk, her sleek platinum hair not daring to move out of place. "And I lost half my life savings in the process. You can decorate the club with as many nude statues and erotic paintings of flowers as you want, Summer, a new relationship doesn't even begin to tempt me. What about you, Brianne? Are you looking for a Mr. Right Now tonight?"

Not yet. She was more interested in keeping an eye out for a Mr. Wrong from her ancient past. Rumor had it FBI agent Aidan Maddock was investigating the scandal that had rocked the club last year, and he was the *last* man Brianne needed to see. Sure, Aidan might have held more than a little appeal for her at one time, but the man held a grudge against her stepfather and had proved himself impervious to Brianne's every seductive machination ten years ago. He'd be better off remaining in her past.

But Brianne wasn't entirely comfortable with spilling her intimate thoughts to women she'd only known for all of a month. "I'll be too busy doing my job."

Keeping an eye out for the agent she suspected would be watching Club Paradise very carefully. "Speaking of which, I've got some security concerns I'd like to share as soon as Giselle arrives—"

"Sorry I'm late." On cue, the club's head chef, Giselle Cesare, burst through the office door. A petite, dark-haired Italian-American, Giselle was a nonstop bundle of energy. She balanced a tray of exotic drinks topped with fortune cookies in one hand. "I thought the start of our new venture deserved a toast." She lowered the tray of drinks on to the desk with a flourish. "Introducing the Good Fortune Potion, newest specialty of the house."

While Summer squealed, Brianne hurried to stuff a glass in Lainie's hand. Lainie was having a difficult time getting over the fact that her husband had not only embezzled half her money, he'd also indulged in a quick affair with Giselle before he'd skipped town. What Lainie didn't seem to understand was that the bastard had hurt Giselle nearly as much in the process, providing her with more guilt than a guileless twenty-five-year-old deserved. Giselle had had no idea that the man had been married.

But even Lainie seemed to catch the momentary spirit of camaraderie and she sipped at her drink, too.

"This is awesome." Brianne raised her glass to the chef and temporary bartender. "But before we toast the grand opening, I wanted to suggest we open our doors a little earlier than we anticipated to try and minimize the crowds out front. There are already journalists swarming and I don't want our guests getting hassled about the club's old scandals.'' Nor did she want to miss her stepfather's nemesis, agent Aidan Maddock, if he tried to get in the disco tonight.

Lainie and Summer were both shaking their heads before she finished. Lainie set her fortune cookie on a cocktail napkin atop Brianne's shiny lacquered desk.

"We want the press, Bri, even if it's negative,'' she argued. "And we definitely don't want to lose the long line out front as that's one of the main elements of cachet for a hot spot.''

"Not to mention the moon is void of course until almost eleven tonight,'' Summer added, clutching one of her crystal necklaces as if for good luck. "We agreed to open at eleven because by then the moon will be entering Aries and the stars will be in a favorable position for the new venture.''

Brianne focused very hard on her fortune cookie to prevent herself from rolling her eyes. "But it's difficult for the surveillance cameras to detect images with the bright lights of the television crew glaring into their lenses. I'd hate to have a security breach our first night because we failed to take a few simple precautions.''

Brianne recognized the importance of security measures. Her last relationship before she'd left New York had been with a guy who couldn't seem to take no for an answer. If not for her techno-gizmos and stepped-up security measures, she might have actually been concerned for her personal safety. Did it hurt to be a little careful?

"I could send some of my erotic pastries out to the TV group,'' Giselle offered, tapping one short, efficient fingernail on her glass. "That might distract them a little longer until we're ready to open the doors."

"Send some of the Kama Sutra cookies," Summer urged, "those pretzel positions ought to keep the crew intrigued for at least another hour."

Lainie shook her head. "I wouldn't want to waste her most delicate work on the *media*." She sniffed in distaste at the word. But then, all of the members of Club Paradise's new ownership had been scrutinized in the news over the past few weeks. "I think most of the reporters are male, so I bet a box of the doughnuts with cherry nipples ought to be distraction enough. Good thinking."

Brianne exchanged surprised glances with Summer. The compliment was the most civil exchange Giselle and Lainie had managed all month.

"Is that okay with you, Bri?" Lainie asked.

"It ought to work. Heaven knows I wouldn't want to disrupt our moon timing."

"We all want tonight to be a success, don't we?" Summer asked, unoffended. "A little help from a favorable celestial alignment couldn't hurt."

"Neither could a toast," Brianne agreed, lifting her Good Fortune Potion high in the air. "To the success of Club Paradise."

"To a feast for the senses," added Giselle, clinking her glass in time with her words.

Lainie rose to her feet. "To a fat bottom line and sweet, financial revenge."

Summer sidled over to the group. "And for crying out loud, girlfriends, let's have a little fun while we're at it. May we all enjoy the single life at its absolute, delicious best.''

Their collective clank of glasses sent Good Fortune Potion spilling down their arms and to the floor as they christened their partnership and began a friendship.

1

THE PROMISED FORECAST of raining men had turned into an outright downpour. Too bad Brianne couldn't seem to enjoy all that testosterone right now.

She slipped away from the sizzling salsa beat and raucous voices in the disco's Moulin Rouge Lounge to seek the privacy of her office. Not only because she'd never been that much of a party girl, but also because she took tonight's job seriously.

After the Rat Pack embezzlement and the difficulties the new ownership had faced getting Club Paradise back on track, Brianne wasn't about to risk any security breaches to land them in tomorrow's newspapers. From the safety of her high-tech office haven, Brianne could survey lovers' quarrels on the dance floor or catfights near the ladies room—anything with the potential to attach more scandal to the club's name.

She'd be damn sure nothing happened on her watch. Not with her entire life savings wrapped up in the club now.

Her finger settled over the mouse on her computer to click through the security monitors in the unused portion of the hotel. There shouldn't be any activity in the resort rooms tonight, just empty scaffolding and paint cans that were part of Summer's massive decorating overhaul.

She clicked on autopilot, zipping through the views of the former Sweethearts Suite, the Lovebirds Nest and the excessively gilded Honeymoon Heaven. She was about to flip screens back to the lounge when a movement in Honeymoon Heaven caught her eye.

Instantly alert, Brianne pressed a few more buttons to tell the camera to zoom in on a shadowy figure crouched beside the bed. Nerves tense, she waited as the lens refocused and lightened the picture at her command.

Lo and behold, the dark shadow slowly rose from the floor and turned into a huge bear of a man. Standing at a good six-foot-four, he dwarfed the delicate white, heart-shaped bed. His dark hair reached his collar, a bit overgrown and as tousled as if he'd just crawled out of bed with an overenthusiastic woman. A short Fu Manchu beard-mustache combo gave him the trendy-scruffy look of South Beach.

He wore a Harley T-shirt with jeans that had seen better days. Reflective sunglasses perched in his hair even though it was well past midnight.

And for the second time in her life, Brianne thought he was the most unusual-looking FBI agent she'd ever seen.

After ten years, Aidan Maddock hadn't changed a bit.

Her heart jumped a bit out of rhythm as she stared at the object of her eighteen-year-old fantasies. She'd half expected to see him tonight, given his unrelenting pursuit of her ex-stepfather's criminal activities. Did

Aidan really think she'd be hiding her crooked old man under the bed in the Honeymoon Heaven?

She needed to get him out of the club. And she would go confront him. Soon.

For now, she couldn't resist another minute or two to just look her fill. She'd wondered during her years working in the film industry in New York if she'd imagined how intriguing-looking Aidan had been.

She hadn't.

Perhaps it was merely the producer-director in her that so enjoyed watching the way his big body moved, the way he dominated his environment at every turn. But her accelerated breathing led her to think her reaction had very little to do with her work as a director.

And everything to do with being a woman.

He looked utterly out of place in the white room overflowing with lace and gold accents. He picked up a miniature music box in the shape of an old-fashioned woman's boot and poked at it with one large finger.

The absurdity of the gesture reminded her that she'd always thought they'd be a great match because Aidan would overshadow a more delicate woman. At five-foot-eleven, Brianne had never been a fragile flower.

Silly, romantic thinking of an eighteen-year-old.

Dismissing the notion, Brianne flicked off the camera zoom and prepared to confront Aidan in person.

Until one of Club Paradise's new employees sidled across Brianne's monitor screen and insinuated herself in front of Aidan. Brianne recognized the cigarette girl from the Moulin Rouge Lounge. A definite fragile flower, the young woman had wide blue eyes and sort of fluffy blond hair. She looked innocent as a damn baby chick, but she was probably close to the age Brianne had been when she'd fallen hard for Aidan.

Only Aidan looked at this newcomer with considerable more interest than he'd ever shown Brianne.

Not that she cared. It was a purely detached observation. Something Brianne had gotten very good at during her years spent in New York. After her overly dramatic childhood with a temperamental mother and a charming, white-collar criminal stepfather, Brianne had become a quick study in detachment.

Scooping up her handheld computer, she switched the picture from the Honeymoon Heaven camera on to the miniature device so she could keep tabs on the action while she walked through the club to the resort's tacky white room. Aidan hadn't needed to pick any locks to get into the suite, but he was definitely treading where he shouldn't have been by ignoring the signs saying Employees Only.

For that matter, the cigarette girl was way out of line, too. Brianne would tell her that as soon as the elevator reached the top floor.

As soon as she shoved open the door and—

Real life collided with the image on the monitor as Brianne walked in on Aidan and the cigarette girl in a liplock to set a woman's heart racing. The stacked little blonde pressed every one of her considerable curves against Aidan and practically climbed her way up his tall body.

Brianne lounged in the door frame, determined not to allow any stray feelings to tangle themselves up in what needed to be accomplished here.

Instead, she steeled herself against the sultry overload of hormones in Honeymoon Heaven and took command of the room in her best director voice.

"Am I interrupting something?"

AIDAN MADDOCK HAD BEEN waiting to hear that throaty purr all night.

He hadn't particularly wanted to hear it while he had Daisy Stephenson clinging to him like a honeysuckle vine.

Luckily, Brianne Wolcott had the kind of take-no-shit attitude that even a little rebel like Daisy respected. She leaped off him like a scared rabbit and scampered out of the room before he could discreetly thank her for her minimal spying efforts this week. He paid her to be an informant, not a sexual booby trap, but he'd have to wait to explain that until next time they met.

Now, he needed to focus all his attention on Brianne as they were suddenly very alone.

"Nice to see you again, Brianne." Aidan mentally scrambled to cross swords with the stepdaughter of his recurring nemesis. The same man who'd been at the root of his first-ever FBI case had eluded Aidan and half the police force in Dade County. He would need to be on his toes tonight if he was going to gather any useful leads. "You look…" Hot. Sexy. A hell of a lot better than he'd even remembered. "…great."

Understatement of the year. The body that had already been slender and seductive at eighteen was worthy of its own pinup calendar ten years later. Her stark black skirt and blouse were slim-fitting and simple, accentuating the sleek, elegant curves of her body. With her long auburn hair and creamy pale skin, she possessed the hot-to-trot attributes of one of those too-cool female cartoon characters in a kick-ass video game geared toward guys.

Not that he ever wasted his time playing video games or anything.

She snapped her handheld computer closed. A half smile kicked up one corner of her soft, peach-colored lips. "Thank you. Although I can't imagine you're finding it all that nice to see me since I've not only busted you in an off-limits zone, but I also caught you with your pants down." She let her gaze wander southward to his jeans. "Figuratively speaking, at least."

The supercharge jolt to his libido was immediate and dead-on accurate. If Daisy Stephenson was a sexual booby trap, Brianne Wolcott was nothing short of dynamite.

He whistled, low and long, like a kettle hissing off steam. "You left Miami as a sweet young thing with big dreams, and now you come sauntering back like hell on wheels. What exactly did those New Yorkers do to you, Bri?"

She tilted her head against the door frame, obviously unruffled by his observation. "Nothing I didn't want them to. Now, are you going to leave quietly, Maddock, or am I going to have to call security?"

She used to be so damn sweet. So trusting. She'd been naive enough to trust *him* when he had been gunning for her stepfather in a federal case ten years ago.

"Come on, Brianne. We both know the extent of your new security team is you. For now, at least. Why don't we sit down and catch up for a few minutes instead? You can tell me all about your stepdad's latest scheme.'' Bottom line, he was here on a mission.

He needed information on Rat Pack ringleader Mel Baxter, a slick crook with a knack for pulling off big scams and walking away clean. After Aidan's investigative efforts had failed to produce enough evidence to convict Baxter a decade ago, Aidan's professional reputation was riding on this investigation. He did not need a so-sexy-it-hurts woman from his past fogging up his brain cells.

Brianne straightened in the doorway and strolled closer. Her black outfit clashed with the sticky-sweet white lace fabrics in Honeymoon Heaven. Aidan realized he was tracking the progress of her hips with his eyes and ruthlessly wrenched his gaze upward.

''I made the mistake of having loose lips around you once before, Maddock.'' She stopped just outside his personal space, leaving him all of six inches to breathe. ''And I guarantee it's not going to happen again.''

His jaw tightened along with every other movable body part. What sort of freaking perversity made it impossible not to want a woman who declared herself off-limits?

He should have felt ashamed at her obvious reference to the one time he'd slipped up and returned her enthusiastic kiss in those last months before she left for New York. But all he could feel was overwhelming curiosity about what it would be like to be on the receiving end of a kiss like that now.

''Never say never.'' He had to keep this conversation light, nonconfrontational if he ever expected to cultivate Brianne's help. God knows, he needed a break somewhere if he was going to catch up with his quarry. "Haven't you heard it's dangerous to tempt fate?"

"Is that a warning, Agent Maddock?" She leaned fractionally closer, getting in his face as boldly as any sparring partner he'd ever encountered. The tough-girl effect was mitigated, however, when a sexy strand of auburn hair slithered out of place and fell forward over one shoulder.

"Just a little friendly advice from your local FBI guy, that's all." He tried hard not to imagine what it would feel like to run his fingers over that shiny red curl. And failed. "Because I like you, Brianne, I'll give you another tip. You'd be doing yourself a favor if you let me know when Mel gets in touch with you."

She rocked back on her heels, the first sign she might not be as cool, calm and collected as she wanted him to think. Her eyes widened just a fraction before she pivoted away.

Aidan's professional instincts went on high alert. "He hasn't already tried to contact you, has he?"

Brianne flipped open the miniature computer she'd been carrying in one hand and checked the tiny monitor screen. "I'm not certain I'd be discussing it with you if he had. But rest assured, I don't want anything to do with Melvin and he knows it. He's my *ex*-stepfather, and he has been for a long time, remember?" She closed the computer again and her gaze connected with Aidan's. "Look, I don't have time to escort you to the parking lot since I've got to get back to work. I just came up here to tell you to get out of my business and don't come back."

She edged around a half-erected piece of scaffolding and headed for the door.

"Wait, Bri—"

"Oh, and because I like you, Aidan," she turned when she reached the gilded archway of cherubs and vines that led to the hall, "let me give you a little friendly advice."

Hell, this meeting had gone so abysmally, maybe he ought to be taking advice from the crook's daughter. He folded his arms and waited.

She cocked a hand on one gently curved hip. "Next time you want to pull a covert snooping mission, why don't you choose a room that's *not* under camera surveillance?"

Aidan would have liked to have argued he hadn't been trying to be sneaky. But of course, that would have been a flat out lie. By the time his gaze discovered the tinted panel in the mirrored ceiling, Brianne's high heels were already clicking their way down the Moroccan tiles of the hallway floor.

Didn't that go over well?

He was supposed to be investigating Florida's biggest thief of the last decade yet he waltzed in here tonight making rookie mistakes left and right because Brianne Wolcott was involved in his case.

Sure, he'd *wanted* Brianne to find him tonight—he'd needed to talk to her. But he hadn't meant for her to discover him kissing the cigarette girl or to record his antics on film. His mistake in not noticing the camera panel ought to damn well teach him not to wear sunglasses past dusk.

Brianne had been right. She had, without a doubt, caught him with his pants down.

But not for long. Aidan might have been surprised at the level of awareness she sparked in him, but next time they met, he'd be prepared. He'd think about baseball while he spoke with her, if that's what it took to safeguard against inappropriate thoughts.

He was going to have a *real* conversation with Brianne now. A talk that didn't involve sexual innuendo or past recriminations. A talk that focused solely on his case.

Chucking his shades in a cupid-covered trash can on the way out the door, Aidan rooted around his brain for enough baseball trivia to stifle all sexual thoughts while he talked to Brianne. As if *that* were possible.

He could read *Baseball Weekly* cover-to-cover and not find enough to distract him from mile-long legs and her I'm-in-charge strut.

Nevertheless, as he made his way through the lobby toward the offices at the back of the club, he started ticking off slugging percentages for the whole Marlins' roster.

OBVIOUSLY, BRIANNE HAD been immune to the Good Fortune Potion. Having the FBI show up her first night in business definitely equaled bad mojo. Especially when the guy with the badge happened to be the object of an embarrassing ancient crush.

She wound through the darkened resort lobby on her way back to her office, all the while wondering why the federal investigator assigned to her smarmy stepfather couldn't have been fifty and balding. Or a woman. Or even a guy who looked remotely like a Fed was supposed to—sharp suit, regulation haircut, clean-shaven.

Instead, she got all six-foot-four of non-conforming Aidan who looked more like a Hells Angel.

Sighing, she slipped into the safety of her office and cursed her predilection for rebels. Hadn't she learned anything from dating that psycho guitarist in New York? Sure, his tortured music had appealed to her as a fellow social outsider, but maybe she should have taken the electric-blue highlights in his hair at face value. Jimmy had been out of control.

Not bothering to flip on the light, Brianne checked her monitors and slid out of her shoes, padding silently around the glass-and-mirror studio in her bare feet. Summer had puzzled over how anyone could work in an environment so coldly sterile, but Brianne had never been one to reveal too much of herself. She preferred her remote haven to the raucous party taking shape on monitor number one.

She turned up the volume on the video feed from the stage camera in the Moulin Rouge Lounge. The floor show was just getting underway with dancers in white-feathered headdresses that were far more elaborate than their skimpy costumes. Yet as Brianne absorbed the images of half-dressed women striking deliberately erotic poses, all she could think of was the even more enticing video in her possession.

The archived footage of Aidan Maddock prowling around Honeymoon Heaven.

Assuring herself she only wanted to look at it for a minute, Brianne flicked the appropriate switches on her control panel until the cupid quarters flashed up on the main screen. The gilded white room was vacant now.

Maybe Aidan had realized Club Paradise was exactly what the new ownership purported—a legitimate business out to recoup the losses of its former incarnation. All the women involved in rejuvenating the scandal-mired resort either wanted a chance to make back the money they'd lost when the Rat Pack left town, or they wanted an opportunity to prove themselves career-wise. Some of them were hoping for a little of both.

Brianne rewound the archived footage until she found the moment Aidan entered the room—only about five minutes before she'd discovered him. She smiled in spite of herself as she watched him in action. Instead of breaking out his fingerprint kit or high-tech phone tap equipment, Agent Maddock had pumped six quarters into the hospitality cabinet to earn himself a Milky Way bar that was probably a year old.

Then, as if testing the mattress, he'd bounced on the heart-shaped bed for a minute before peering into every nook and cranny of the saccharin-sweet accommodations.

Her gaze drank in the sight of his rangy body. He'd been that tall ten years ago, but his frame hadn't been quite as solid. Muscles filled out his Harley T-shirt now, stretching the well-worn fabric in a way that made Brianne's mouth water.

No doubt about it. Aidan Maddock still sizzled her from the inside out and no amount of her in-your-face bravado was going to change that.

She just hoped to God Aidan would never realize as much.

No sooner had the thought occurred to her, then the office door swung open behind her. An awful premonition flitted through her mind—a scenario she did not want to contemplate as she stared up at the big-screen version of sexy Aidan Maddock.

Please let it be Giselle with another round of Good Fortune Potions. Or maybe it was Summer ready to yell at her for watching television in the dark again.

Please let it be anyone except...

"Looks like you couldn't wait to see me again after all." A far-too-cocky voice filled the studio. A masculine bass that definitely hadn't originated on her tape.

...Aidan.

2

BRIANNE REACHED FOR the remote to pause the videotape, but Aidan's hand beat hers to the control.

"I'll take that." He swiped the electronic device behind his back, allowing the tape of himself to continue rolling. "I want to see the part where you walk into the room. I've never seen anyone make an entrance quite like you, Bri."

The man could be all charm when the situation warranted. No wonder she'd fallen for him a lifetime ago.

Good thing she knew better now.

"My entrance isn't until after Daisy's." Brianne tried not to notice when the curvy blonde sashayed her way across the television screen in her micro-miniskirt. "But by all means, enjoy the show until then. You wouldn't want to miss the footage of your lip lock."

Aidan hit the pause button on the remote, stilling the picture on the television just as Daisy entered Honeymoon Heaven.

"Actually, I'm not here for the show. I'm here to discuss Club Paradise."

Brianne stiffened, recognizing the FBI-guy tone creeping into Aidan's voice. "If you want to talk business, maybe you'd better make an appointment."

"Does that mean if I want to talk personal, you'll listen to me now?"

Was it her imagination, or had he somehow moved closer? The heat of his body warmed Brianne's purposely sterile office. If she let him stay in here long enough, she had the feeling he could single-handedly steam all the mirrors and glass.

"I'm saying, make an appointment." She held out her hand for the remote. "Can I have my equipment back? I'm trying to run a smooth operation here tonight—a fact you seem to be repeatedly forgetting."

But Aidan was already walking away from her, keeping her remote hostage in the back pocket of his jeans. Damn the man.

Of all the places she wouldn't touch, he couldn't have picked anywhere more off-limits.

"You're pretty interested in technology gadgets, aren't you, Bri?" He trailed a finger across her master control board, an action that drove techno-types as insane as nails on a chalkboard.

"Touch my buttons and you're dead, Maddock."

"Seems like I'm already hitting all your buttons." He gave her a wicked grin and dropped into a black leather chair in front of the control panel. "Seriously, I heard you studied some major technology while you were at film school. I thought you'd always wanted to be a director?"

With his big body sprawled across her office furniture and his thinly disguised nosy questions, Aidan might as well have hung his FBI shingle on her front door. Despite his lazy posture and casual approach, Agent Maddock was clearly at work.

Brianne sighed, sinking into the leather chair beside his. She didn't stand a chance of getting any work done until she'd answered at least a few of his questions. "I am a director. As I'm sure a professional snoop like you already knows. I just happened to enjoy the engineering aspect quite a bit."

His gray eyes held hers a second too long, reminding her of the best kiss of her life....

"You always were into electronic contraptions, weren't you? Remember that remote key finder you gave me?"

Her cheeks warmed. Did he *have* to remind her of her schoolgirl crush on him?

She frowned, hoping maybe he'd think she gave useless widgets to everyone she met.

"It's the envy of every Fed in my office," Aidan continued, oblivious to her discomfiture while he warmed to his topic. "I left my keys in a Chinese restaurant once and that remote led me right to my beeping key chain. Of course, I had to dig through a little chow mein in the back alley to retrieve them, but it beat walking home."

Brianne blinked, surprised at the genuine appreciation in his voice. "I've progressed since then," she found herself saying before she could question the wisdom of sharing anything about herself with this man. "Now I can program a menu into my refrigerator so that it reminds me what to take out of the freezer every morning."

"You're kidding." He looked at her like she'd just solved one of his cases. "You ought to work for the

Bureau, Brianne. Sort of like Q in those James Bond flicks.''

She had to admire his skillful way of bringing the conversation back around to business. Frankly, she welcomed the distancing reminder of their opposite worlds. She'd been enjoying their conversation just a little bit too much. ''Joining the Bureau isn't going to make me start spilling secrets about Melvin Baxter. I have no idea where he is.''

His gaze met hers as she denied it, as if he was subjecting her to some sort of mental lie detector test.

''Do you think your mother has been in contact with him?'' Aidan leaned forward in his chair and pulled her remote control out of his back pocket to study it, as if he didn't place much importance upon her answer.

Brianne saw straight through the act. Aidan took his job seriously and he was on a mission tonight. She couldn't buy into his cool FBI guy with a Fu Manchu facade this time around. Aidan might look laid-back, but she knew firsthand he tracked down his personal ''most wanted'' with single-minded focus.

''I don't know, Aidan. Even if I did, I'm not certain that I'd discuss it with you.'' Too much ancient history between them. Too much hormonal short-circuiting if she sat within touching distance. ''Now, can I have my remote back? I've got work to do.''

He lifted one dark eyebrow, a quirky expression Brianne remembered well. Her eighteen-year-old self had tried for at least half an hour to raise only one eyebrow like that, and she'd ended up with a massive headache.

''And you think you can just snap your fingers and

make the FBI disappear?'' Aidan pitched the remote from hand to hand, never taking his eyes off her.

While she admired the man's dexterity—and didn't that give rise to intriguing questions about what else he did well with his hands?—Brianne couldn't afford to allow him to distract her with his sleight of hand.

She snatched the device away from him in midair. ''I might not be able to make you vanish this minute since I'm working solo tonight.'' Besides, he didn't exactly pose an immediate danger the way a drunken patron could if she took her eyes off the screens. ''But I *do* know I'm entitled to go about my business while you're here. Either cut to the chase about what you want from me, Aidan, or let me do my job.'' She pressed a button on her recaptured electronic controller and flipped through several camera feeds to monitor the action throughout the club.

Of course, she needed to then follow through on her action and swivel in her chair to view the various monitors off to her side. A position which left her staring up at several small televisions along with an oversize, frozen image of Aidan and the cigarette girl, Daisy, on the middle screen.

She had larger-than-life Aidan on camera in front of her, and all-too-real Aidan emanating pheromones behind her.

A pretty powerful combination.

Good thing Brianne had gotten over her crush on him long ago or this situation might have presented a problem.

A shiver tripped through her while she waited— hoped—he'd give up. Maybe he could go search for

Daisy Stephenson's mouth again. Surely anything would be better than just sitting there behind her.

She could feel the weight of his stare along the back of her neck. She was also pretty damn sure she felt every one of his 98.6 degrees heating the boundaries of her personal space.

And he was getting closer.

Brianne didn't know how she knew it, but the hair on the back of her neck stood on end with awareness. To turn around would be like acknowledging her curiosity. Something she definitely did not want to admit—even to herself.

But what *was* he doing back there?

TWO HOME RUNS IN THREE at bats.

Aidan rallied his quickly-splintering concentration to keep his mind off Brianne and his hands to himself.

Think baseball.

The Marlins' first baseman had been on fire last night—moving his slugging percentage up to almost seven hundred, if Aidan's math proved semi-reliable.

Which it probably wasn't, given that the usual appeal of bases gained divided by at bats couldn't compare to the allure of Brianne Wolcott's auburn hair spilling over her barely-covered back.

Pale, satiny skin begged his touch while her killer strawberry curls shimmered in the reflected light of ten different televisions.

He might have persevered and calculated stats for the next guy on the roster if only Aidan didn't remember exactly how smooth that creamy skin felt and how intoxicating her exotic scent had been from their long-ago, accidental interlude.

The faint perfume teased him even now, urging him closer to indulge his memories of Brianne.

As he leaned forward, his hand brushed a button on the elaborate master control board. The oversize screen in front of them came to life in response, setting Daisy Stephenson in motion again.

Saved by the cigarette girl.

Aidan pressed himself back in his seat, as far away from the temptation of Brianne as possible. What had he been thinking to let himself get so close?

Brianne pivoted in her seat, a half smile on her face. "Ready for your big screen debut?"

He welcomed the cool distance in her voice. Hell, he needed an Arctic blast to stay focused on business with Brianne around. He settled for jerking a thumb toward the television, confident his limited exchange with Daisy on screen wouldn't reveal the woman's connection to the Bureau. Brianne's tape didn't include the audio feed she had for some of the others.

Daisy had been more interested in jumping him than providing information.

"Maybe you can give me a few pointers on how I did." Aidan needed an excuse to hang out with Brianne, some time to build a rapport with her again.

"Are you sure you can handle an assessment of your technique?" She folded her arms and peered down her nose at him, the ice queen in full battle mode.

Luckily, Brianne's cool demeanor had never scared him off.

"Since when have I had an ego problem?"

She cracked a genuine smile, a gift all the more special because it was—in Aidan's experience—so rare.

"You've got me there." She turned back toward the screen just as Daisy flung herself into Aidan's arms on the archived footage. "Prepare to be critiqued."

Aidan scooted his chair forward to sit side by side with her, telling himself an essential part of his job was building relationships with people who might have key information on his case. His gut told him Melvin Baxter would be in touch with the ex-stepdaughter he'd always doted on, and Aidan was going to be there when it happened.

His job—his whole badass reputation within the Bureau—demanded it.

His decision to sit two inches from Brianne had absolutely nothing to do with the fact that he wanted a better whiff of her perfume.

He stole a glance at her in the dull blue glow radiating from the wall of monitors. Some of the televisions caught the action on the dance floor, around the bars and in the back alleyway. But Brianne stared up at the video of Daisy and Aidan, head tipped to one side as if trying to make sense of the film sequence.

"You bumbled this kiss from the beginning." She pointed one pale pink fingernail toward the central screen. "It's all awkward angles and bad timing."

"That's not my fault. I got cast with the wrong woman."

Brianne snorted, her gaze glued to the image of Aidan being clawed into submission by the voluptuous informant.

Okay, maybe he hadn't exactly fought the woman off. But she'd taken him totally by surprise.

"I'm serious," he protested, wishing his first meeting with Brianne after ten years didn't have to take place during a fluke lip lock with an overeager coed. "I'm a foot taller than this girl. I need a leading lady with some major long legs."

He couldn't help but smile as Brianne strutted her way into the video scene right on cue.

"Weak excuses. You'd never make it in film, Maddock, no matter how much you flex those ripped muscles."

Her eyes widened, almost as if she'd said more than she'd meant to. Aidan couldn't help the slow smile that crept across his face.

She snatched up her remote and smashed the pause button. "Now, I think we can both agree I've humored you tonight. It's time you either get to the point of your visit or you're really going to have to leave."

Shit. Aidan needed more time to convince Brianne he wasn't the devil's spawn she seemed to think him. Then again, maybe all the time in the world wouldn't be enough to convince her she could trust him.

One botched encounter with her that night before she left for New York and he ruined the great connection they'd once had.

Unfortunately, it was time to play hardball because he sure as hell couldn't walk away from his one and only lead to Melvin Baxter.

"Actually, I'm going to have to carve out a spot for myself at Club Paradise for a little while, so we might as well try to work together." He scratched an idle hand across his chest, affecting a casualness he definitely didn't feel. He flexed his bicep for her benefit. "You really think the muscles are looking ripped?"

He would have been golden if he could have teased another one of those killer smiles out of her. But as he met her stormy green gaze, he was pretty sure there would be no smiles forthcoming.

In fact, he was damn certain he was about to experience the brunt of Brianne's new hell-on-wheels attitude.

A COLD, CLAMMY FEAR SETTLED in her gut, but Brianne would rather be cut off from her remote for all of eternity than let Aidan know. He wanted to settle in *here?* To work?

That could only mean the FBI had her under a microscope, a notion which scared her right down to the silver rings on her toes. If word got out the new club was being investigated, it would taint the place with an underworld feel she and her partners were working hard to overcome.

Thankfully, she'd learned a thing or two about acting in her time behind the camera as a documentary producer, and it wasn't that much of a stretch to work up some annoyance at Aidan's presumptuous, self-absorbed shtick.

"I'm not about to get into a discussion of your physique in light of your earlier comment." She met his gaze levelly, hoping no barroom brawls would break out at the club in the moments she took her eyes off the security monitors. The scene inside her office promised to be more explosive anyhow. "What exactly do you mean you need to carve a spot out for yourself at Club Paradise?''

He leaned back in his chair as if utterly at ease with the notion, then laced his fingers over his reclining chest. ''Melvin pissed off a lot of people with this latest stunt, Brianne. You know he took off because we were ready to nail him with racketeering charges?''

No, she hadn't known. Didn't want to know. She'd said goodbye to Melvin and all her mother's other shady—but well-providing—boyfriends and ex-husbands ten years ago. Brianne was well into a new chapter of her life now.

Thoughts of Jimmy the guitar player niggled in the back of her mind. Had she somehow started her own parade of shady boyfriends?

''That doesn't have anything to do with me or with Club Paradise.'' She stood, eager to walk away from the implied intimacy of the darkened room and the proximity of their seating arrangement. She flipped on all the overhead lights, determined to chase away all traces of shadiness in her life. Starting now.

''Whatever business Mel was running out here, it's not going on anymore. The women I'm partners with have so much collective fury at the Rat Pack that we could probably take down all of them if they were ever stupid enough to set foot in South Beach again. But they're not. Mel is gone and he's going to stay gone.''

Aidan blinked against the sudden deluge of high wattage filling the room. ''And you think you can make it so by the sheer force of your will? Mel has connections all over town and a strong racketeering operation in place. He's not going to walk away from that income forever.''

Why had her mother ever married such a loser?

Bad enough Pauline Wolcott-Baxter-Menendez-Simmons unabashedly married the men for money. Did she have to be so unconcerned with how they made it?

Brianne leaned against the master control board, strung tight and wishing she could appear half as at-ease as the agent lounging in her office chair. She set the remote control on the panel beside her. ''He knows better than to contact *me*.''

''I disagree. And since I'm running this investigation, that means I'm going to hang out at the club, watch the surveillance cameras with you, and generally be your best friend for the next few weeks.''

Like hell. ''I don't think so, Aidan. One of our owners is an attorney, you know. If there's a way to legally keep you out of here, Lainie will find it.''

He rose, unfolding his six-foot-four frame from his slouchy position in the chair.

To Brianne the subtle physical message couldn't have been more obvious. He was no longer talking to her as an old friend. He was issuing FBI-guy orders in no uncertain terms.

''I don't think Lainie is going to find an easy opponent in the justice system, Bri, but good luck. In the meantime, I'll be here tomorrow night before you open.'' He drifted closer, his shuffling walk landing him a scant foot from Brianne.

She had to look up at him to meet his gaze. One perk of her height was that she usually got to meet men eye-to-eye. She could have gained a couple of inches if she'd pried herself off the soundboard perch, but that would have put her much too close to Aidan.

"I'm not showing you my videotapes without a search warrant." By God, she was going to lay down some rules here, too. If Aidan thought he could blithely walk through her door and charm her into doing whatever he wanted, he was dead wrong. She'd learned the hard way not to put her trust in this man.

"Why? So I can't see the drunken three a.m. crowd pissing on the sidewalk on their way out of the club? Or so I can't see the floor show for free? If Melvin's not going to contact you, what do you care if I sit here and watch your tapes with you?"

That was the whole damn point. She didn't care what he *saw,* she cared that he'd be sitting two feet away from her all night, every night. Besides, she needed to show him he couldn't waltz back into her life and expect he could manipulate her like some infatuated teenager.

"Bring a warrant or you don't see a damn thing." She'd hold her ground on this one.

"Fine." Nodding, he conceded her point. "But I'm going to be all the more demanding about what you have to show me if I go to the trouble of getting the paperwork."

She scavenged up a few remnants of her New York attitude, the facade she'd needed to make it in the city's competitive film industry. She leaned close enough to whisper, her chest hovering inches from his.

"Demand all you want, Aidan. I don't think you'll be able to obtain a warrant for what you *really* want to see."

If there were any justice in the world, the fact that Aidan chose that moment to lick his lips would mean Brianne had the power to make his mouth go dry.

An idea that pleased her to no end.

"Good thing I don't need the court's permission for that particular show." He picked up the remote control and pressed play, starting the footage of their meeting in Honeymoon Heaven. "Why don't you sit down and watch the sparks fly between us on camera and then try to tell me we're not going to end up seeing a whole lot more of each other before this investigation is through?"

He shoved the remote into her hands and headed toward the door.

And despite the staggering number of New York film producers she'd mouthed off to in her day, she couldn't think of a single comeback to Aidan's preposterous suggestion.

He turned at the door to shoot her a parting grin. "See you tomorrow, Bri." He lifted one eyebrow in signature Aidan style. "But only as much as you are ready to show me, of course."

Damnation.

As he disappeared into the hallway, Brianne wondered how she'd survive the next go-round.

Somehow she'd dropped a sexual gauntlet tonight and Aidan Maddock hadn't wasted any time picking it up. If she was going to maintain her sanity over the next few weeks, she needed to get her mind off those mouthwatering muscles of his and back on her job.

Because Brianne had already revealed too much of herself to Aidan ten years ago, and she didn't have any intention of making herself vulnerable to him again.

3

BRIANNE SLID FARTHER into the gurgling outdoor hot tub, allowing the bubbles to tickle her nose as she held her glass out to Giselle for more champagne.

To celebrate their first night in business, Club Paradise's new owners had agreed to meet after closing for a soak under the stars in one of the many oversize tubs surrounding the main pool. Amid wafting steam and the thrum of the bubble jets, the four of them were sharing stories from trenches. Summer had lost one of the dancers' outfits and the woman had trotted out topless, Giselle had gotten into an argument with a drunken patron who insisted she didn't know how to make a proper Sex on the Beach, and Lainie had a run-in with the cigarette girl over leaving her station in the middle of the evening.

The last part came as no surprise to Brianne, of course.

Brianne raised her glass for a third toast, wishing she didn't have to share her bad news with the happy celebrants. She smoothed a slick finger over the painted ceramic tiles on the rim of the hot tub, pausing on the image of a towering pagan god in the Atlantis-themed picture. The golden god's knowing expression reminded her too much of a certain cocky Fed. She covered the picture with her beach towel, obliterating the pagan with Egyptian cotton, and decided she couldn't keep her news a secret any longer.

Shoving a damp curl out of her eyes, she cleared her throat. "On a less happy note, we received a visit from the FBI tonight."

Giselle choked on a sip of champagne while Summer nearly spurted hers across the pool.

Barely managing to swallow her beverage, Summer slammed her glass down on the ceramic tiles. "You're kidding."

"Unfortunately, I'm not. Remember the guy I told you about who's been chasing down Mel forever?"

"Aidan Maddock." Lainie sat up straighter, tense and wary. "He questioned me after Robert disappeared."

"Me, too," Giselle added, casting an apologetic look at Lainie. "And I'm used to huge, intimidating males with those brothers of mine, but I thought Maddock was totally scary. What did he want?"

"He pretty much told me he's going to become a regular fixture at the club until he uncovers a lead to the Rat Pack. Mainly Mel."

"Oh great." Summer saluted the idea with a nearly empty glass. "We'll attract lots of business with a Fed at the front door. Did you at least inform him our bouncers don't wear three-piece suits?"

Lainie held out one manicured hand for attention, sort of Barbara Streisand style. "Maybe it's not such a bad thing. I mean, pardon me for sounding like a bitter.divorcée, but wouldn't we all rejoice just a little if every one of the sleazeball Rat Packers got carted off to federal prison?''

Summer and Giselle, both of who had been dating former part owners of the business, looked ready to agree.

''But at what cost to the resort?'' Brianne retorted, staring up at the stars as if there might be some answer contained in the limitless indigo sky.

And, a little voice inside her asked, at what cost to herself?

''We didn't even know he was here tonight,'' Lainie replied, plucking up her glass again as if the matter was settled. ''As long as he sticks to the shadows, he's not going to be chasing away business. Sure, we're inconvenienced now, but in the long run, if this Agent Maddock catches the cheating bastards who ran Club Paradise into the ground, so much the better.''

Giselle and Summer were quick to raise their glasses to that sentiment.

Great. Brianne slid deeper into the tub and wished she could slink away from this problem as easily. Even her own friends thought it was a good idea to hang out with the only guy who had ever broken her heart.

Brianne sighed, but she toasted the plan along with everyone else, silently agreeing to help Aidan with his investigation.

She just hoped he could solve his case quickly because she had a real problem with men who tried to push all her buttons.

THE SOUTH BEACH STRIP was kicking into high gear by the time Aidan found an empty parking space near

Club Paradise the next night. The club wouldn't open for another hour, but he wanted to stroll through the grounds, get the lay of the land before he crossed swords with Brianne again.

Thanks to her and her knack for sexual innuendo, Aidan hadn't slept the night before. Her implication that he wanted to see more of her had been dead-on accurate and his mind had obligingly created an image of naked Brianne for Aidan to drool over until the crack of dawn.

Now, tired and irritable, he faced the prospect of sitting next to her all night with as much enthusiasm as a suspect being read his Miranda rights.

Good thing Aidan knew how to focus on his job. As long as he ignored the sexual chemistry between him and Brianne, he'd be fine.

Winding his way through the palm trees and vacant cabanas on the resort's flawless beachfront property, Aidan made mental notes of the terrain and tried not to remember he hadn't been able to ignore the chemistry thing with Brianne when she'd been all of eighteen.

How could he ever pretend he wasn't attracted to her now that she was every bit a consenting adult?

Well, maybe not completely consenting. Yet. Damn it, why did he keep thinking she *might* be if he applied a bit of effort to the task?

Tugging open a tinted glass door to one of the resort's four connecting Mediterranean-style buildings, Aidan welcomed the Arctic blast from the air-conditioned interior. He'd been overheating from more than just the sultry Florida air.

A pop tune blared from the disco, bouncing through the marble and tile hallways to the small reception area between the hotel and the club. The sound would be more muted once carpets were installed, but for now, Aidan was subjected to a warbling soprano belting out bubble-gum lyrics along with the reigning pop princess who sang over the speakers.

Curious to see the source of that brazenly out-of-tune voice, Aidan peered into the club to find two women congregated with Brianne at the end of the low stage and a colorful blonde with braids in her hair sashaying down the runway like a model for hippie-wear. Her see-through skirts were layered so you couldn't truly see through them, but the effect was intriguing, especially given their rainbow hues.

The singing woman taking center stage provided a perfect foil for austere Brianne on the sidelines in a chocolate brown, sleeveless cat suit. Brianne looked like a jewel thief ready for her next heist, minus only a ski mask. Her every move was elegant, her tall body as quietly graceful as the blonde was noisily ostentatious.

"Well, who do we have here?" The blonde stopped in mid-chorus, drawing the gazes of the three other women toward Aidan.

He could sense the slight stiffening of Brianne's already perfect posture, feel the thread of tension emanating from her.

She laid down the clipboard she'd been holding, but she didn't exactly run over to greet him. "Summer Farnsworth, say hello to Aidan Maddock, our very own federal agent."

Brianne reminded him of the other women's names. He'd questioned them both after Melvin and company took flight. The blonde on the runway stared down at him with unmasked surprise.

"*You're* the FBI guy?" Her gaze roamed over his backward baseball cap and his white T-shirt that advertised a regatta from three years ago.

"That's me. But I'd prefer if we kept that as low-profile as possible. Sort of an undercover thing." He turned to Brianne and nodded toward the doorway. "Can I bother you for a few minutes?"

He needed to get this initial face-off with Brianne behind him so he could move on with his investigation.

She didn't answer, but she picked up her handheld computer and sauntered toward the door, long legs perfectly outlined by the slim fit of her outfit.

Aidan took the opportunity to stage whisper to Brianne's friends, "If anyone asks, I'm her new lover. It's part of the cover." Could he help it if his work provided fun perks?

"I heard that," Brianne called over one shoulder, not even pausing as she plowed through the doors toward the hotel.

Aidan nodded to Brianne's partners before he followed her, thinking he'd probably need to investigate them a little more fully. Summer Farnsworth and Giselle Cesare seemed like face-value women, but Lainie Reynolds might have a few things to hide. She'd been married to Robert Flynn, Melvin's closest partner, when the Rat Pack had pulled out of South Beach.

Of course, he wasn't thinking about anyone but

Brianne by the time he caught up to her slim silhouette strutting down the hall toward her office.

"Wait up, Bri."

She had obviously inherited the New York pace while living up north.

Brianne spun on him in the middle of the opulent corridor. Perfectly centered under a massive crystal chandelier, she stared him down and began her advance. Her high heels clicked an ominous tone on the Moroccan tile floor as she closed the space between them.

"If I'm going to allow you to invade my life over the next few weeks, don't you think you could at least do me the courtesy of keeping up with me?"

She looked pissed, and he would guess that didn't have anything to do with him not keeping up with her. Still, some demon drove him to provoke her.

"But how are we going to perpetuate the idea that we're a couple when we can't even stroll along side-by-side?"

The spark in her green eyes practically burst into flame.

"And how dare you put me in a position of having to look like your..." She gave him a thorough once-over, as if she couldn't believe she'd have to attach herself to him even if it was only in rumors. "...*lover*. Did it ever occur to you I might object to such a ludicrous cover story?"

"You really think it's ludicrous?" He peered down at his three-year-old regatta shirt, wondering if she had a point. Brianne definitely looked more uptown than Aidan ever would.

She continued to advance, backing him right into a marble table beneath a mirror the size of a swimming pool.

Not that he was complaining. He finally got a whiff of that perfume that had teased his nose all last night.

Sort of musky and dark. Almost as if she'd gone out and bought a bottle of sex stimulant and spritzed it on her neck.

"It's utterly preposterous. Daisy, for one, is going to see right through it given that you were *her* lover just yesterday." She pointed a finger dead center at his chest and held it a fraction of an inch from his sternum. "You could have told them you were my neighbor, my brother, my mechanic or my decorator, Aidan. Any of them would have been more plausible."

"Your decorator?" He wasn't totally certain he'd heard her correctly. He was too busy taking small breaths so the aphrodisiac she used as perfume wouldn't bring him to his knees.

"Yes. My decorator." The idea made her smile. Not the real Brianne smile, but the half-cocked version that made her look like a sultry pinup girl.

Okay. He was a politically correct guy and all. And he was pretty sure there were plenty of heterosexual male decorators in the world. But from the wicked gleam in her eyes, Aidan would stake his badge she was trying hard to insult him.

And she was doing a damn good job.

"But I bet I can pull off a convincing kiss a hell of a lot better than I can hang wallpaper." He inched forward just enough to back up his claim.

Her eyes widened. The finger she'd been jabbing at

him fell to her side. She even backed up a step before regaining her take-no-crap attitude.

"Don't forget I critiqued your kisses, Maddock." She pivoted as if to continue toward her office, deeper into the vacant recesses of the luxury hotel. "I wouldn't be too sure how convincing they can be."

Ten years ago, she'd melted in his arms so fast he'd almost forgotten she was just barely legal. He ground his teeth, knowing a gentleman would *not* remind her of the way she'd reacted the last time he'd kissed her.

But damn it, some sort of reminder was definitely in order. He would have easily squelched that seldom-used gentlemanly conscience if only he didn't need to make some serious plans for his stakeout tonight.

Instead, he settled on a surprise move that served both his purposes. Catching up to Brianne's hell-on-wheels walk, Aidan slipped an arm around her to halt her in her tracks.

He leaned close to her ear to speak, close enough to feel the rapid-fire pounding of a pulse gone rogue.

"Wait a minute, Bri," he breathed against the shiny silk of her hair.

Right away, he knew he'd made a big mistake touching her. Not only did that brief contact fog his brain on the details of an investigation that had seemed so important two seconds ago, but having Brianne in his arms—even just for a moment—also made him start to rationalize ways he could instigate a hot, no-holds-barred encounter with her and still be true to his case.

An ill-advised thought at best. A surefire road to disaster at worst.

She remained perfectly motionless, almost as if she was afraid to breathe for fear of touching him any more. "What are you doing?"

He would take his hands off her any second.

Soon.

"I'm steering you in the other direction." And proving to her she wasn't totally immune to him, maybe.

Too bad what started out as a bid to save his ego had just bitten him in the ass.

He no longer had any idea who was proving what to whom. But he knew exactly how much he wanted Brianne right now.

"My office is this way." She managed to say the words without moving an inch. "Along with all the surveillance equipment."

Aidan needed to explain he wanted a walk-through of the whole property first. In his mind, he told her exactly that.

In reality, he breathed deep enough to get the full effect of her sex-in-a-bottle perfume.

In reality, he spread his fingers and thumbs a bit farther apart on her waist to cover a little more territory.

And in reality, he knew he didn't stand a chance of letting go without just one taste.

IF AIDAN HAD TRIED a frontal approach, Brianne would have been prepared.

She would have fended him off with a few well-chosen words, maybe another decorator crack, and she would have been on her way to her office right now.

She hadn't counted on this sneak offensive from behind.

Funny thing was, now that she stood so close to him, encircled in his arms and surrounded by enough muscle to bench press her several times over, Brianne didn't feel like fending him off.

To fight against an attraction that had plagued her since high school seemed foolish. And damn it, she hadn't spent ten years in New York's balls-to-the-wall film industry only to run away from a little confrontation.

She'd take what she wanted from Aidan and move on. Follow the heat right into the fire of the kiss she wanted so badly and then get on with her life. Nothing like tackling your demons to excise them.

Aidan had started this sultry interlude. But *she* was going to finish it.

Right here, right now.

She didn't give him a chance to retreat. Turning in his arms, she faced him in the deserted hallway, stared up into eyes she'd seen in more dreams than she could count.

But instead of allowing Aidan to come to her, as he always had in her overactive imagination, Brianne rose up on her toes to meet his lips with her own.

Consciously, she choreographed the moves as carefully as if she were behind a camera directing the action. This was not a kiss to indulge in for selfish reasons. This would be a tongue-tangle with a mission. Not only would Brianne demolish her old infatuation with Aidan, she also intended to wipe all memory of Daisy Stephenson from his mind while she was at it.

Her hands smoothed over his white T-shirt, appreciating the sculpted perfection of his body. Her fingers twined in his hair, tripped along the back of his neck.

He tasted like toothpaste and Tic Tacs—minty but warm. She anchored herself to him, savoring every inch of his hard masculine planes next to her soft, compliant curves. She couldn't have molded to him any more perfectly had she been made of Play-Doh.

It would be a challenge to break away from the heat of his body, the seductive taste of a kiss she had been waiting ten years for. But she had no choice.

She *had* to walk away from him.

And then *he* touched *her*.

Perhaps she'd been so absorbed in playing out their kiss just the right way that she hadn't noticed he wasn't participating fully.

Until right now.

Aidan's hands cupped both her hips, steering her exactly where she needed to be between his legs as they stood in the hallway. Brianne didn't dare open her eyes to peek at their reflection in the swimming-pool size mirror because she had a feeling the image of them pressed together would be too erotic to bear.

But then, keeping her eyes closed proved to be an incredibly sensual experience as well. Without the distraction of her sight, Brianne seemed all the more in tune with her other senses. The slight evergreen scent of his soap mingled with the fragrance of her perfume, the heat of their bodies amplifying the normally subtle smells.

Aidan's hands continued to hold her prisoner through pleasure. He ran his palms up her shoulders and outlined her collarbone with his fingers. The palms of his hands hovered a scant inch above her breasts, making them tingle and tighten in response.

But more intoxicating than anything else was the

wet slide of his lips over hers. His tongue teased and tasted her, made her a full participant in her own seduction.

She could feel herself swaying on her heels, recognized the approach of a sensual tidal wave sure to drag her under. Still, she couldn't take her hands off Aidan if she tried. Her fingers moved with restless energy over every available inch of him, cataloguing the shape and feel of his chest through his cotton shirt. She pressed him as close as possible to the needy greed of a body gone too long without a man.

Every ounce of her energy went toward remaining on her feet or she might have ended up sprawled across the Moroccan tile with Aidan Maddock.

Instead, a shrill rendition of a pop anthem reached their ears.

She was saved by Summer's bad taste in music.

Brianne broke away, still reeling from the out-of-control mouth mating. Her heart slammed against her ribs as if she'd sprinted a mile. She simmered with need, her body on fire for more.

But she couldn't let Aidan know. The man had already refused her once. She would make sure he never had that opportunity again.

It required every shred of her limited acting ability, but Brianne found her motivation in a hurry.

Aidan could *never* be a part of her life.

"That wasn't too bad." She fluffed her hair and called up a smile for Aidan's benefit, hoping her knees wouldn't cave right underneath her in the wake of that kiss. "Maybe all you needed was a little practice."

4

THE KISS HAD OBVIOUSLY fried Aidan's neurons because no way in hell could he have understood what Brianne had just said. Then again, blood blasted through his veins as if his body was fuel injected, so maybe he just couldn't hear over the rush of red blood cells. And the warble of off-key soprano down the hall. "Run that by me again?"

Brianne cocked one hand on her hip, the hall mirror behind her reflecting the stance with an even more interesting view. Her green eyes stared him down even as her lips still trembled from their tongue tangling. "I suggested your kiss was a credible effort. But now I propose we move on to business and quit with the spin-the-bottle games. If you want my help, Aidan, you can't try to downplay your mission with questionable charm. We both know what you're really here for."

Aidan took a step back, his hands raised to shoulder height to show her he meant no harm. The woman was hot as a pistol—just fired and smoking. He needed to start exercising a little caution around her or they were liable to both get burned.

He had no business kissing her or touching her. No right to prove that her tough-girl guise was all an act. He had the feeling that with another touch—maybe two—he and Brianne would find out exactly how much heat was left in their attraction to one another.

But he couldn't afford to get wrapped up in her now. Not with his case riding on her cooperation and his residual doubts about her innocence in Mel Baxter's shady dealings still looming.

"You think you know what I'm really here for, Brianne?" Right now, he was wondering himself. Sure, he needed to put Mel Baxter away as a matter of professional pride. Mel was swindling half of Miami by now, but Aidan still held a grudge that the guy had made off with half his grandparents' life savings ten years ago when Mel dabbled in television evangelism.

His grandmother and grandfather had managed the monetary loss, but they'd never gotten to enjoy their retirement.

Still, Aidan didn't have any idea if he was standing in Club Paradise right now because of them. Or because of all the Dade County bigwigs who'd lost money investing in the resort.

Aidan wondered if, deep down, he'd hightailed it over here tonight to see what it would be like to kiss twenty-eight-year-old Brianne as opposed to eighteen-year-old Brianne.

No comparison.

The woman must grow more potent with each passing year.

"I know exactly what you're here for since you made it very plain to me yesterday." She swiveled on one high heel and continued in the direction of her office, her shoes clicking a fast beat on the colorful corridor tiles. "You want access to the club and you want to view my videotapes. That won't be a problem assuming you've brought the necessary paperwork.'' She paused in her sexy strut. Turned her head in a way that sent auburn hair swishing over her shoulder. ''You do have a warrant, don't you?''

Of course she wouldn't forget about that. Aidan had known better than to think he could roll right over Brianne Wolcott.

''About the warrant—''

She folded her arms across her chocolate-colored cat suit. The bare skin on her arms looked far softer than the expression on her face. ''Forget it. No warrant, no tapes.''

Shit.

Aidan had practically begged a federal judge for the warrant in addition to presenting credible evidence for why he needed access to Brianne's security archives. According to his informant, those cameras of hers had been running for nearly two weeks. Who knew what evidence they might have captured in that time?

But the judge was a notorious hard-ass and hadn't been impressed. Leaving Aidan with nothing to sway Brianne other than his smooth-talking charm.

And from Brianne's tight-lipped glare, Aidan suspected no amount of cajoling would help him in his cause tonight.

''I couldn't get the warrant. But it's just a damn piece of paper, Brianne. I need to be here if I'm going to find Mel.'' His voice was loud enough that his words bounced around the wide hallways and tile surfaces.

''To you it's just a piece of paper, maybe. But it's

a legal necessity to me.'' Brianne's voice whispered along the corridor, but her message was every bit as clear. "Contrary to your beliefs, I don't have anything to do with men who circumvent the rules at every turn. I'm on the straight and narrow, and you need to be, too, if you expect me to cooperate with your investigation.''

Aidan skimmed a hand over his baseball cap-covered head, willing a good idea to pop into his brain before Brianne tossed him out on his ass. He needed to be here tonight. Call it gut instinct. Intuition.

But something told him Club Paradise held the keys to Mel Baxter's whereabouts and Aidan's case.

No way could he allow Brianne's anger at him from a decade ago to overshadow his number one priority.

"If I leave the club tonight, Brianne, I can guarantee you I won't be far away. And I won't really be gone." He took a step closer, ready to go toe-to-toe with her on this. He lowered his voice, unrepentant about using mild intimidation tactics on a woman who could probably teach him a few things about attitude. "Wouldn't you rather have me in your sights so you know where I am and what I'm doing as opposed to having me in the shadows, watching you when you are unaware?''

He hadn't meant to infuse the question with sexual overtones, but as the words left his lips the provocation was suddenly just *there*, not even remotely subtle.

Brianne didn't betray a thing with her cool expression, but Aidan watched her shoulders rise and fall with the same bracing breaths he was taking to keep his hands in check.

Damn, but he wanted to touch her again.

"Surely you aren't supposed to coerce innocent people in the course of your investigations, Agent Maddock." In the background, the blaring pop music finally ceased. "Are you certain your superiors would approve of your approach?"

Hell no. But then again, Aidan had never advertised himself as a play-by-the-rules kind of guy. Sure, his unorthodox methods had landed him in the agency's doghouse sometimes, but they had also accounted for a stellar track record on his cases overall.

"Maybe not. But if you don't mention the coercion, I won't dispute your status as an innocent person."

Before Brianne could reply, Aidan heard the double doors of the club open out on to the corridor several yards behind him. Feminine laughter and a collection of clicking high heels approached.

"I'm a hell of a lot closer to innocent than you are," she hissed between clenched teeth, no doubt attempting to hide their conversation from her advancing business partners.

"You must have a short memory, Bri," he whispered back, only too pleased for the excuse to lean closer to her. "The steamy propositions you tossed my way as a wild eighteen-year-old were more inventive than any I'd heard before or since."

BRIANNE HAD SPENT the last ten years cultivating a proficient poker face to negotiate with the heavy hitters in her male-dominated profession. But she had the feeling that—despite her best effort—her expression now was nothing short of panic-stricken.

She'd suspected Aidan would remember a few of

the racier proposals she'd issued in her overeager youth. But she really, *really* hoped he wouldn't remember one in particular.

A fantasy of hers—ancient, of course—involving Agent Aidan Maddock in his investigator role and Brianne in her suspect role.

Specifically, a strip search.

Cloaking any sign of her fears with an effort, Brianne recovered just as Summer, Giselle and Lainie reached them.

Summer flashed a thumbs-up as she cruised by in her rainbow-colored skirts and braids. She was a walking fashion emergency today but she still managed to look gorgeous. "I tested the club microphones in your absence, Brianne, and I'm happy to report they are working just fine."

Giselle settled for winking at Aidan as she tapped past them too, but Lainie paused and donned her cool, face-the-public smile for his benefit.

"Agent Maddock, I trust Brianne has explained to you that all the partners behind Club Paradise are happy to extend our full cooperation to your investigation of the former ownership?" Lainie smoothed an already perfect strand of her blond hair behind one ear, her gold cuff bracelet glimmering in the lighting from an overhead chandelier.

Brianne sighed inwardly at her co-owner's helpfulness.

Aidan responded with the full force of his charm. "Thank you, Ms. Reynolds. Brianne was just getting ready to give me a tour of the resort so I could get acclimated for making myself at home here over the next week or two.''

Had he told her he'd be here for that long?

''Excellent. Just let me know if you need anything else.'' Lainie smiled with more efficiency than warmth, and it occurred to Brianne she probably hadn't ever seen a full-fledged grin on the new CEO's face.

One day she'd ask Summer more about Lainie's story, but now as her partner departed down the hallway, she was too annoyed with Aidan to think about it anymore.

Aidan turned on her, his mask of polite good humor vanishing. His dark brows flattened into a fearsome slash across his forehead. ''Care to tell me why you're wasting our time arguing about whether or not I have your authorization to hang out on the premises when your partners have obviously already agreed on it?''

Unwilling to be cowed by the tough-guy act, Brianne decided the time had come for a little cold, hard honesty here.

''Has it ever occurred to you I might not want the object of an ancient and embarrassing crush glued to my side for two whole weeks?'' She struggled to keep her tone even, level. Her work had taught her that women were more likely to be written off if they emoted too much. Men had the luxury of acting out when and if they so chose, but thanks to an age-old stereotype of the hysterical female, women had to pull the ice queen facade in order to make men take them seriously.

Usually, she was superb in that particular role. But oddly enough, the subject of Aidan Maddock still had the power to get her a little more riled than she cared to admit.

Aidan frowned. "You find an old crush on me embarrassing? You think I've gone downhill in the last ten years, Bri?"

A little exasperated sigh broke free.

After ten years of keeping her cool—even with the psycho guitar player former boyfriend—Brianne couldn't believe Aidan was already getting under her skin.

"That's not what I mean and you know it. I don't appreciate having to rub elbows with a guy I once threw myself at as if I were—"

"Some kind of lovelorn teenager?" he supplied.

She glared at him. "Some kind of blind and disillusioned kid."

Aidan nodded. Placated her. "You're right. I can see where the situation might be a little awkward for you." Was he hiding a preening male smile underneath that pseudo-charm of his? "But now that we've established that I'm going to be welcomed here by the rest of the owners, why don't we move on to a quick tour of the grounds and then I'll make myself scarce."

"Then you don't need to be in my office with all the security equipment?" If she'd known they didn't have to be together all the time—

"I meant I'd make myself as scarce as I can be in your office," he amended quickly as he made a sweeping gesture for her to go first down the hall. "I'm pretty damn good at my job, you know. And the faster I find out where Mel is hiding, the sooner I'll be out of your hair."

"I can't help you there," Brianne protested, though she knew Aidan didn't believe her any more now than he had a decade ago. Not that it mattered any longer. "But I can give the tour of the property in less than an hour assuming you can keep up."

She blew by him, grateful for the distance her long legs could cover in just a few paces. And she didn't wait to see if he followed.

This time, Brianne would be the one leaving him in her dust.

AIDAN TOOK A SHALLOW BREATH as he sat shoulder to shoulder with Brianne at her master control board later that night. A deep breath would draw in too much of her scent, too much of her. And he was already edgy and restless from spending half the day glued to her side.

They'd only been apart long enough for Brianne to change out of the sleek brown cat suit she'd been wearing and into a skirt short enough to leave him practically drooling in her wake. Apparently this new outfit was the kind of getup a woman wore when she worked in a nightclub.

Getup being a pretty damn descriptive phrase at the moment.

Now, she stared up at her wall of monitors and spoke softly into her headset to one of her partners. The blue digital clock on the control board turned to 4:00 a.m.—closing time—while she narrated a drunken man's actions to the party on the other end of her connection. It sounded like Brianne was asking if she should intervene in the situation.

Aidan could hardly keep quiet. "If he doesn't make it out the door under his own power in another minute, I'll run him off." He didn't like the idea of Brianne playing bouncer to a two-hundred-and-fifty-pound biker with spikes strapped around his wrists. Besides, it would probably do him some good to get a breath of air that didn't involve Brianne's darkly complex perfume.

Brianne covered the mouthpiece of her headset with one hand and glared at him in the dim light of the security board in her office. "I don't think so, Maddock. Thanks anyway."

Had she always been this bristly? Even now in her crisp white man's shirt and shorter-than-short black sequin skirt, she had a cool, hands-off look about her before she said a word.

"You're running a one-woman show here, Bri," he shot back as he switched screens on the monitors to check out the action on the street in front of the club. Still no signs of Mel Baxter. "Can you really afford to turn away offers to help out?"

"I can when they come from a man who's only interested in dragging the club's name through a little more mud." She uncovered the mike on her headset and told her partner she'd check in later then clicked off the connection.

"I offered to kick out a drunk. You don't have to make a federal case out of it."

"*You* obviously want to." Brianne tossed aside her headset and opened the top of her computer display. "That's the only reason you're here, after all—to make your federal case and then ride off into the sunset a hero. Of course, it doesn't matter to you that you could be costing four women their livelihoods and their dreams for the second time in one year. As long as you get your conviction, who cares what happens to the club, right?'' She spared him a glance over her shoulder, her red hair dancing around her shoulders like a fitful flame as she moved. ''So do me a favor and don't pretend to care what happens around here before you pull the rug out from under us.''

She went back to tapping away at her computer keys, her breathing measured and regular and totally unruffled while he was still over here choking on his freaking shallow gulps of air so as not to inhale too much of her damn mess-with-his-head perfume.

The whole day had been an exercise in professional and sexual frustration. Mel's trail was cold—possibly thanks to his stepdaughter's smooth maneuverings— and Aidan's superiors grew more agitated with the situation with each passing day. And instead of focusing on his work, Aidan was more in tune with Brianne's every movement in the chair beside him, every breath she took and every slow uncrossing and recrossing of her mile-long legs.

He'd watched video camera feeds of half-naked women shimmying across the stage in the Moulin Rouge Lounge all night, their painted nipples poking through the white feather bras they wore with their white skirts. Brianne, on the other hand, was encased in a forbidding expanse of starched white dress shirt, yet he could envision her breasts more clearly.

And as if that weren't bad enough, he'd been plagued by memories of her long-ago racy propositions ever since they'd finished their exploration of the hotel and plunked into their seats in her office.

When she'd been giving him the grand tour, she'd shown him the tacky Sweethearts Suite decorated in chocolate brown and pinks, the bedspread a nightmare of bright candy wrappers and peppermint sticks. Instead of thinking like an agent and gleaning details to apply to his case, Aidan had been swamped with a vision of eighteen-year-old Brianne in her candy striper's outfit asking him if he wanted to see her tie a cherry stem with her tongue.

No doubt about it, Brianne had been a wild child.

And while Aidan had congratulated himself at the time for ignoring her overtures—repeatedly—all her suggestive propositions were coming back to him in vivid color. Only, he wasn't remembering the Brianne of a decade ago issuing them.

In his mind's eye, he was hearing them come from the Brianne of today.

The Brianne with the take-no-shit attitude and the sexy saunter that could bring a grown man to his knees.

And it was driving him insane.

Steeling himself for another round with her, he shoved his chair away from the control board and swiveled his seat to face hers. "I can't afford to care about the consequences of Mel's arrest. Chances are they're going to up his status to one of Florida's most wanted men if I don't bring him in within the week. Do you think criminals shouldn't be punished just because it might have a few negative effects?"

Brianne shoved away from the control panel and stood. "Of course not. I'm just saying don't pretend to give a rip about the club or me when you're doing your damnedest to run us both out of town.''

Aidan shot out of his seat, putting them inches apart.

So maybe it wasn't such a great idea to confront her, he thought as the perfume that had been teasing his nose all night wafted even closer.

If her body was even half as hot as his, no wonder he could smell the scent all the more.

"I'm not trying to run you out. Or your business, or your partners. As long as you're not helping him cover his tracks, lady, you've got nothing to worry about.'' He didn't want to think about Brianne being involved in anything illegal. But she had remained close to her stepfather for years after he'd divorced her mother.

Aidan knew because he had Mel's file practically memorized.

Brianne turned her back on him to glide her way across her office floor, her high heels barely making a sound on the brand-new black industrial carpet. Every facet of the woman's space was coolly functional and austerely impersonal. No photos, no frills and no nonsense for this woman.

Aidan could relate. He'd gone the frills and sentiment route with a woman five years ago and look what had happened.

Disillusionment on both sides. Disappointment. Divorce.

Aidan wouldn't be treading down the path of vulnerable women anymore. He'd tangled with innocence and had ended up hurting his wife with his dangerous job, his total cluelessness when it came to sensitivity.

Brianne, on the other hand, knew the score. As she

stood there in her black sequined skirt and her all-business white shirt, Aidan couldn't see a hint of vulnerability in the woman.

And innocence?

Brianne might protest her innocence in a courtroom, but she had to know as well as he did that she liked living on the edge. She was no stranger to danger or adventure.

Even though Aidan had been too much of a gentleman to indulge her eighteen-year-old sensual urges despite her provocation, he had no doubt that she'd been able to lure other men to her bed. And had probably left them begging for more and ruined for any other woman to boot.

No, Brianne Wolcott hadn't been vulnerable *or* innocent for a very long time.

Which meant she was the kind of woman Aidan allowed himself to touch. To take home. To satisfy mutual urges.

He tracked her movements on the other side of the room—this woman who was distracting the hell out of him. She was talking to him as she flipped through papers on her desk. Apparently she'd been telling him off while he'd been caught up in his own lust.

"...and I don't care what Lainie says," she was saying, eyeing him with a sharp green gaze. "Negative press does not equate with good publicity as far as I'm concerned. The club has enough association with the underworld. I have every intention of making this place a success despite Mel and all his crooked buddies. And despite you camping out here ready to pounce."

She had the right of it in the pounce department.

Aidan's blood was pounding through his head—and through the rest of him—so damn hard he could barely make out her words to him anymore.

There was only one thing left to do to save his investigation. Only one course of action that would rescue him from the constant sexual distraction of Brianne.

He had to have her.

Right now.

Tonight.

It was for the good of his case, damn it. And even though he'd never been a guy to follow standard operating procedure in any area of his life, he wasn't breaking any official rules here tonight. She wasn't a suspect in his investigation.

"I don't know a thing about publicity—positive or negative—so I can't help you there. And I'm sure you are perfectly capable of making this place a success, Brianne, no matter what I do while I'm here." He wanted to take a step closer, but he knew as soon as he did he'd take ten more and then he'd be all over her.

He at least owed her fair warning.

"But that part you mentioned about me being ready to pounce?" His eyes wandered over her with slow deliberation. "You couldn't be more right. I'm guessing you've got about three seconds before I zero in on my next target."

5

BRIANNE COULDN'T HAVE moved to save her life.

Not with Aidan's gaze cruising over her with every bit of sensual heat she'd ever longed for ten years ago. More. She would have never guessed back then that a man's stare could ignite a small inferno.

For that matter, she hadn't known until just this red-hot, blistering second.

If she'd had any doubt about who Aidan's next target might be—she didn't—it was obliterated the second he moved toward her. Invaded her personal space. Crowded her.

This was a bad, bad idea.

Her hungry lips and aching body didn't seem to realize it, however. She'd been too close to Aidan Maddock for the last twelve hours to have any perspective on what she should or shouldn't be doing with him.

By 4:00 a.m., her brain had checked out and her body was moving on pure instinct.

"Does this remind you of anything, Bri?" His voice was close. Too close.

He bracketed her body with his arms, steadying himself on the wall behind her.

She gulped for breath but only managed to inhale the scent of Aidan.

If she wasn't careful, she'd be lost in a tide of sensation and her own desire. She licked her lips in a vain attempt to make her mouth do something—anything—besides initiate the kind of kiss she had subjected herself to earlier in the day. She'd barely survived the first go-round with Aidan. She'd never emerge from Round Two with her panties intact.

Where was Lainie's Super Glue when she needed it?

Clearing her throat, she fought to keep her voice steady. Even. "It reminds me why we shouldn't get within arm's length of one another. If we're even an inch too close we end up getting drawn together like high-powered magnets."

Aidan flexed his muscles on either side of her, a hard ripple that couldn't help but snag her eye. Brianne shivered in time with the movement. "That's not the right answer. And as a matter of fact, I don't even think it's an honest answer."

"No?"

"No. You can't tell me you're thinking about all the reasons we shouldn't be next to each other right now. My money says you're thinking about all the reasons why one of us ought to take that last little step." He shifted back an inch, giving her a fraction more breathing room. Not enough. "Turn around." His voice went lethally soft.

Brianne's insides turned hot and liquid. The only thing behind her was one mirrored wall.

"But I..." Shouldn't. Couldn't.

Wanted to anyway.

"Do you want to hear what this reminds me of?"

His dark eyes pinned her, teasing her with her own curiosity.

Besides, a dare lurked behind his words and Brianne didn't have any intention of backing down from this man.

Not now. Not ever.

She made a tight turn in the narrow space he provided her, pivoting until she faced the wall of smoky mirrors made all the more moody by the room's blinking blue light cast from ten different television screens.

As she confronted her reflection, Brianne nearly wavered on her feet. She was not a small woman by anyone's standards, yet Aidan Maddock's height made her look almost delicate. Fragile.

His shoulders loomed above hers—broader, thicker. The top of her head reached his mouth, but the expression in his eyes didn't give her the impression he wanted to plant a chaste kiss on her hair. Rather, he looked like a man ready to devour her whole with just the slightest encouragement.

The position—her in front and him behind—didn't make her uneasy. Only…titillated. Edgy. Hungry for whatever it was he had in mind.

When he said nothing, however, a shadow of nervousness shivered through her. "Well?" she prodded.

Aidan's gaze connected with hers in the mirror as he ran his hands down the length of her shoulders and arms. As he reached her hands, he tugged them backward, behind her.

Together.

It was an odd move for him to make. Aggressive. Totally un-P.C. in today's cautious dating community.

But that didn't stop the thrill chasing through her to be held captive by this man.

She watched his reflection in the mirror, noted the way his gaze fell to her breasts that were now thrust forward and pressing—achingly—against her white cotton shirt.

He'd probably spied her lack of a bra at twenty paces given his don't-miss-a-thing federal agent eyes. But if he hadn't noticed then, there was certainly no mistaking it now. Cotton didn't begin to hide the tight peaks from his steamy stare.

"How about now?" His grip tightened fractionally on her imprisoned wrists. "Does this pose spark any memories of a certain fantasy you once shared with me in your bad-girl youth?"

Oh God.

He remembered.

For years Brianne had hoped—prayed—that he'd forgotten the night she'd whispered her naughtiest fantasy into his ear while he sat in his car at a late-night stakeout in front of her home. It had been a last bid to make him notice her as a woman, but it had failed miserably when she realized Aidan had been sleeping on his shift and had missed out on hearing her most forbidden sexual desires.

Or so she'd thought.

Obviously, Aidan had heard every word of her fantasy—muscle-bound cop meets naive civilian and subjects her to a strip search of the most erotic kind.

Brianne wanted nothing so much as to lie. To play innocent and hope he had enough mercy on her to let her off the hook without embarrassing her too much.

But Brianne hadn't been innocent in too many years to count, and she wasn't entirely sure Aidan possessed any mercy.

Besides, her flaming cheeks burning back at her in the mirror's reflection attested to a clear memory of the incident without her even opening her mouth.

Aidan bent closer, his head dipping into the curve of her neck, strategically maneuvering his mouth next to her ear. "I seem to remember it involved some very naughty role-playing."

Her thighs twitched as an ache started between her legs. "A gentleman wouldn't remind me of this."

Aidan swept aside her hair to bare her neck while his other hand kept her wrists firmly in his grip. "Then again, a gentleman probably wouldn't fulfill your most wet and wild dreams, now would he?" His lips met the tingly skin of her throat, then traveled in a slow ride over her shoulder.

Her breasts tightened all the more.

"You're pretty self-important if you think I harbor the same fantasies now that I did back then, Aidan." Liar. Liar.

And God above, were her pants ever on fire.

Brianne could barely stand still as Aidan studied her in the mirror with the slow thoroughness and open hunger of a lover.

"It may not be your fantasy anymore, but you can bet that sweet ass of yours it's been mine for ten years running. You'd better spread those legs if you know what's good for you."

Oh. My.

Air rushed out of Brianne's lungs as the reality of her situation rolled over her.

Ten years after she'd teased Aidan with her sex-crazed schoolgirl daydreams, he was finally giving her what she'd asked for. And no matter that she'd dated a slew of guys since then or had taken a few adventurous turns in the bedroom to satisfy her inner vixen. Her fantasies about Aidan had never totally died.

They'd just been shoved to the back of her consciousness. Until now.

"I'm not the wild thing I used to be," she confided, edging closer to the mirror. "Are you sure you're still interested?"

She didn't say it to be coy. She wanted to make sure he understood she wasn't the same woman who had proposed all those crazy sexual schemes to him a decade ago.

But Aidan's knee was already wedged between her thighs. "I said spread 'em."

He let go of her hair and grazed one hand over her starched shirt to rest on her abdomen. Right above the place she burned for his touch the most.

The whole situation was out of control along with her body. This wasn't good for her personal peace of mind or her professional association with the club. But closing time had come and gone and she wasn't on the clock anymore.

She'd worry about the consequences of her actions tomorrow. Hell, she was an expert at cleaning up from the fallout of her ex-stepfather's shady dealings and her mother's life dramas. Why shouldn't she use all her sweep-it-under-the-rug skills for her own benefit for a change? Surely she could find a way to make this problem go away.

Tomorrow.

Right now, all she needed to do was lock the door and forget about everything except this one fantasy come to life.

Wriggling her hands against Aidan's grip, she met his gaze in the mirror. "The remote on my wrist can lock the office door. Two keys from the right on the top row."

Behind her, Aidan's fingers worked the button and then slid her master remote control from her wrist. He tossed the device on the desk a few inches away. "The door's locked." He peered up at the wall of television screens behind them. "Your drunk is even now stumbling his way home up Ocean Drive and your club is closed for the night. You don't have any excuses to keep you from complying now."

Actually, she did have a few reasons. But she didn't feel like thinking about any of them when Aidan's body hovered an inch away from hers.

She edged her legs farther apart.

Aidan stared down at her thighs in the mirror. He used one foot to nudge her stance even wider until her slim-fitting sequin skirt strained just a little.

She gave him a cool look over her shoulder despite the fire raging between them. "If you're searching me, Agent Maddock, I hardly think you'll find anything under my skirt."

If she was going to indulge this fantasy scenario, she didn't plan to do it in half measures. She would play her role to the hilt.

Not unlike she had one long-ago night when he'd pulled into her driveway while she was in the process of climbing out her bedroom window. She'd teased him then too, shouting down to him while she toyed with the hem of her dress to ask if he thought she was wearing any panties.

His reaction now was far more satisfactory than the scowl she'd earned back then.

Aidan's hot palm moved in small, gentle circles over her belly, totally at odds with the gruff note in his voice. "You'd be surprised what people hide in the most unusual places, lady. And you're pretty high up on my suspect list so you'd better brace yourself for thorough inspection."

Apparently, Aidan was sliding into his role pretty easily too.

A layer of steamy mist fogged the mirror, clouding their reflection to a hazy shadow. But Brianne didn't need the reminder of what she looked like in her wanton pose as Aidan's prisoner. The image had singed itself into her memory forever.

"I know my rights," she taunted him, leaning more heavily into his thigh that was still lodged between hers. "And you can be damn sure you won't get away with this. By tomorrow, you'll be paying for these liberties you're taking."

The hand he rested on her abdomen slid into action, molding her starched shirt against her body. His fingers slid between the buttons to unfasten them until he gained entry to her bare skin. Her breasts.

She couldn't help the little sigh of satisfaction that

hissed from her as his callused palm cupped the taut fullness of her.

"Maybe you'll make me pay tomorrow," he admitted as his hips connected with hers, his shaft nudging her bottom with delicious insistence. "But there's not a damn thing you're going to do about it tonight except give me exactly what I want."

AIDAN WAITED, watched for any signs he might be carrying this strip search scene a little too far. He even considered easing up on his grip when Brianne's wrists twisted against his hand.

But then she used her repositioned fingers to stroke over the tip of his cock through his jeans and he felt pretty damn certain he was in safe terrain.

Of course, that was among the least of the things he was feeling right at this moment.

Brianne's feathery caress barely whispered over him in her awkward pose with her wrists behind her back, but that slight touch had an impact that nearly brought him to his knees. Even when she was at his mercy, she still managed to be in total control.

"So what exactly *do* you want?" Brianne arched her back in a way that pressed her breasts more deeply into his hand. She turned her head to one side and then the other, making her hair ripple against his chest like a silken breeze. "Surely you must know I'm unarmed by now."

"I don't know any such thing." He slid her white blouse down her arms, then released her wrists so he could slip the sleeves off. "As a matter of fact, I'm more convinced than ever that you're a dangerous woman with multiple weapons at your disposal.''

He lifted her arms and planted her hands on the mirror in front of her, now too foggy with the steam they generated to provide a reflection. Just as well as far as Aidan was concerned. His lone view of Brianne's body was already nudging him into cardiac arrest territory. If he'd been privy to a simultaneous front view, he'd probably keel over from sensory overload.

Her pale skin stood out in stark contrast to the smoky mirror and her black sequin skirt. A swath of red hair knifed down the middle of her creamy back, a bold splash of color in the austere setting of her office.

She tossed her hair over one shoulder as she turned around to look at him, one delicate eyebrow arched. ''I don't think you can call what I'm armed with a weapon.''

''Splitting hairs on the semantics isn't going to save you from getting frisked.'' He couldn't wait to get his hands all over her. The dark exotic scent she wore curled around them like a fragrant whisper. Her teasing words egged him on in his quest to fulfill her long-ago fantasy even though he was so ready for her he thought he'd lose it any moment.

He needed her now. Wanted her five hours ago.

Still, he planned to take his time patting her down. Starting at the ankle.

Bending low, Aidan noted her black satin high heels. He focused on them narrowly, hoping he could distract himself enough to get through the next few minutes without jumping her.

Her barely-there shoes arched her feet and defined her calf muscles. Fire-engine-red toenails threaded through webs of skinny black straps. A silver toe ring with a tiny red heart decorated her pinky toe.

He concentrated on every curve and nuance of her knees. Her thighs.

Sweat beaded along his hairline. Restraint wasn't easy to come by when confronted with thighs like Brianne's.

Still, as he reached the hem of her skirt, he skipped upward to gently grope her breasts. Her abs. Her hips.

Sequins scraped along the palms of his hands as he eased his touch down her hips. He inched the material of her skirt higher, bunching up the fabric in his hands until she was scarcely covered at all.

His chest pressed against her back. His cock strained against his fly.

And it was killing him not to take her. Right. Now.

Role-playing would be the death of him yet.

He breathed deep. Held it in. Then curved his hand around the inside of her exposed thigh. "I think I've found something here."

Brianne's breath shuddered from her. Her grip on the wall loosened. Her whole body seemed to pool into his touch.

Aidan swiped a hand through the steam on the mirror so he could get a better read on her expression. Eyes closed. Lips slightly parted.

And that was all the invitation he needed.

He turned her in his arms, shoved her skirt down her hips. And holy freaking hell, she wasn't wearing any panties.

Hauling her against him, he slanted his mouth over hers. Kissed her with more need than finesse. She returned the kiss even as she yanked his shirt from his jeans and shoved the cotton up his back, off his arms.

Somehow she'd walked right out of her shoes and she was naked. Brianne Wolcott was naked and wriggling up against him like she couldn't get quite enough.

And he'd thought he was fulfilling *her* fantasy tonight?

This was better than anything he'd ever scripted in his hottest dreams. And he considered himself pretty damn imaginative.

She broke their kiss, her fingers fumbling—enjoyably—with his zipper. "Do you have protection nearby? I have something but it's in a bathroom down a hall and not conducive to—"

"I've got it." He was already digging in his back pocket for his wallet and thanking God for the proximity of a condom. What if Brianne had changed her mind about this in her walk down the hall?

Then again, she seemed pretty committed to tonight as she was already tugging his jeans down his hips. Wrapping her calf around his to steady him as she worked.

Tomorrow he would be adamantly opposed to a take-charge woman trying to steamroll him into doing things her way. But tonight, he was ready to shout with triumph over finding a woman who knew exactly what she wanted and how to get it.

Clutching the condom in one hand, he lifted her up and seated her on the shiny lacquer desk. Because the desk was hers, it was devoid of any decoration, adorned only by a small stack of papers at one end. Aidan vowed to have them scattered all over the black carpet before they were through.

For tonight, he wanted to make her messy, add a little chaos to her smooth perfection.

He shoved off his jeans, his boxers—his shoes were in there somewhere too. He'd sort it all out tomorrow. Right now he just needed to be inside Brianne.

She was kissing his chest, her tongue blazing a hot trail to his shoulder. Her fingers wrapped around his cock, stroked him.

And made him need her all the faster.

He had himself sheathed and ready in two seconds flat. Lifting her off the desk he held her above him. She gripped his shoulders, her short nails digging into him just a little. He celebrated that slip of control on her part, the tiny sign that Brianne was getting caught up in this as much as him.

Then he lowered her. Inch by fantastic freaking inch he eased his way inside her. She was so hot and tight and slick for him he had to bite the inside of his cheek to keep from exploding on contact.

How long had it been since he'd been with a woman?

Not nearly long enough to be this close to the edge already. It was just because this was *her*. Brianne. The woman who'd messed with his head too many times with her precocious sexuality and provocative teasing.

This was fantasy come to life and he was inside her, all around her and breathing her killer fragrance straight from the source.

Aidan gave himself enough mental distance to touch the slick folds where she stretched to accommodate him. He wanted tonight to be burned into her memory, seared into her dreams for weeks, months to come.

He slid his fingers over the heated center of her and took pleasure from the way she shivered and moaned. Not giving her any quarter, he looked for the telltale moments when she bit her lip, arched her back, until she finally yelled his name as she flew apart in his arms.

Mental satisfaction pounded through him. Physical satisfaction hovered, loomed, demanded release. Still, he wouldn't allow himself to hit that high note until he had her settled back on the desk, her creamy pale body stretched out across the slick black lacquer. Only then did he drive into her with the strokes guaranteed to take him where he needed to go.

Brianne's fingers flexed against the desk, her nails scraping the shiny surface until her body bowed with the force of his release. She cried out along with him as he shouted, her hips writhing under his as she moved in time with the last quakes of his body.

And as their voices quieted, their breathing a ragged echo in the room, Aidan watched the last of her stack of papers flutter silently to the floor.

6

BRIANNE LAY BENEATH Aidan on her desk—cold, unforgiving veneer behind her and hot, slightly bristly male muscles above her. Amazingly, she wasn't the least bit uncomfortable. She'd spent half her life between a rock and a hard place anyway.

As hard places went, a girl could do a lot worse than Aidan Maddock's gorgeous bod.

Smoothing her hand over a squared shoulder, she soaked in the feel of raw male power. She'd be willing to bet there weren't many people who'd tangled with this particular federal agent and gotten away with it. Her shady former stepfather was probably one of a very few people—maybe the only person—to get past Aidan.

The thought reminded her of all the reasons she shouldn't be lying here with him right now. Not that she owed her stepfather any loyalty, but she didn't want to get roped into the shoot-out between him and Aidan. There was no doubt Mel was a crook, but Brianne had seen another side of him.

Her mother had gone a little crazy when Brianne's real father had died. She'd spent money like water for months to fill whatever void was in her life and had nearly run them into the poorhouse. Brianne had eaten toast and caviar for two weeks when she was five because that was the only thing her mother had bought to eat. Grocery shopping confused Pauline, but she could tackle Rodeo Drive, Miracle Mile or Fifth Avenue and shower her only child with diamonds and miniature-size dressing gowns.

Not that Brianne had a use for either.

She kissed Aidan's shoulder, savoring the warm heat of him a little longer even as reality was starting to set in again. He shifted away from her and eased off the desk while Brianne closed her eyes and pretended they didn't have to face the consequences of what they'd done just yet. Instead, she reminded herself why she couldn't help Aidan with his case.

Melvin Baxter might be a swindler with little conscience, but he'd marched into Pauline Wolcott's life and made her money worries go away. He'd hired a nanny to make sure Brianne had peanut butter and jelly in her lunch box like all the other kids instead of cold toast and spoiling caviar. And he'd brought her a teddy bear instead of a tiara.

She was glad she didn't know where Mel was now or what he'd done with all the money he'd taken from unsuspecting investors because she'd have a hard time sending the guy to jail after he'd saved her and her mother.

By now Aidan had his jeans back on, though they remained temptingly unfastened. He leaned over her sprawled, naked body, his hard jaw next to her ear.

"If you don't put clothes on, I'm going to be all over you again." His voice was a heady growl, a plea and a threat at the same time.

She believed him. Already she could feel the hard length of him against her thigh. Again.

The thought made her smile. Aidan might have a lock on raw male strength, but he made her feel endowed with a few powers of her own.

''Maybe you'd better give me my shirt.'' Even though her own body was already reacting to his, Brianne knew a second time around with Aidan would only make it more difficult to re-draw their boundaries.

Yet boundaries were non-negotiable.

They were on opposite sides of his case for one thing. His work threatened to cause the deathblow of scandals for Club Paradise for another. And Brianne was through with dangerous men who disorganized her world and didn't know what it meant to play by the rules.

She'd somehow been following a negative relationship pattern with men starting as early as Mel Baxter and winding all the way through her life to Jimmy the psycho guitar player in New York. Aidan might be on the right side of the law, but that didn't make him a straight arrow. He was as dangerous and as rule-bending as every other guy she'd ever been involved with.

She needed to break that pattern right here, right now.

Her body protested the decision even as she slid her arms into the shirt that had already lost its starch. Her breasts still tightened and ached for Aidan. Even though her thighs ached from the fervor of their love-making, Brianne wanted nothing so much as to wrap her legs around Aidan's waist all over again.

The man had been back in her life for forty-eight hours and he was already lambasting her priorities.

As if he could read her mind, Aidan laid a hand on her wilted shirt and splayed his fingers across her hip. "You don't need to rush on my account." His fingers kneaded the soft flesh of her bottom, calling up a deep longing for more.

She gripped his wrist with regret. "But I do. Tonight has to be a one-time occurrence, Aidan, or it will confuse things too much between us."

He leaned closer. "I'm not the least bit confused, Bri. I know exactly what I want."

"But for how long?" She backed up a step and scooped up her skirt off the floor. "When you get a lead on Mel and you can't haul ass out of here fast enough to chase him? You need to walk away from this as badly as I do."

Their gazes connected, locked. Brianne saw the acknowledgement in his dark eyes even if he didn't like it.

Shaking his head, he tore his shirt off the back of a chair and yanked it over his head. "Maybe I do. But I sure as hell don't know how can you just turn it off like that. One minute we're so hot we end up collapsing on to your desk and the next minute you're all starched and untouchable again."

Years of practice, that's how.

But Brianne wasn't about to share any more of herself with this man tonight. Her boundaries were already too fractured and weakened for her to walk into that tenuous territory of pillow talk with a man like Aidan.

She needed to reinforce the walls and then do a little

hauling ass herself. Wrenching her skirt up her legs, she explained her position to the best of her ability. "I can't afford to let minor setbacks compromise the overall goal."

Judging from Aidan's slack-jawed expression, however, she guessed her explanation was a bit lacking in his eyes.

He seemed to recover himself and jammed his feet into his shoes. "So let me get this straight, Ms. Sentimental. You and your scientific brain have classified tonight as a minor setback?" Lifting his baseball cap from its perch on her master control board, Aidan shoved the hat on his head. Backward. "In that case I'll do my best to stay out of the way and not compromise you or your damn goals any more. You're all heart, Brianne."

He didn't bother looking back as he stomped his way out the door, leaving Brianne with a little remorse, an aching body, but thankfully, what heart she possessed was still very much intact.

And Brianne, for her part, intended to keep it that way.

AIDAN HAD TO HAND it to her.

The woman had a hell of a lot of nerve.

He parked the Harley in front of a restaurant on Ocean Drive with killer coffee and tables on the street that overlooked the beach. It wasn't one of the trendy joints where the European models hung out to smoke cigarettes and chug java, just a run-of-the-mill steak-and-egg place where a guy could eat real food and still keep one eye on the street.

He intended to hole up at a private table and stuff himself with greasy hash browns until he forgot all about Brianne calling their night together a minor setback. Until he forgot all about her come-hither stare and her sexy-as-you-please strut.

Fat chance.

If nothing else, he just needed to get some mental space away from her perfume and figure out where to go with his case next.

But his wish to be alone crashed and burned as he spied his former college roommate, now an up-and-coming Miami attorney, Jackson Taggart, flagging him down from a table along the front row. Aidan's usual table.

Damn.

Normally he saw Jackson twice a month for a round of golf—Jackson's sport of choice—or a day of fishing—Aidan's preferred Sunday activity. If Jackson had skipped his morning workout to hunt down Aidan, chances were Jackson needed a favor.

"Look what the cat dragged in," Taggart called by way of greeting. As was typical for Jackson, he wore a tie at 7:00 a.m. His suit was crisp at sunrise, and Aidan would lay money the pleats in his pants could still cut through butter at midnight. No doubt, Brianne would love this guy. "I haven't seen you this mauled over since college. You putting in late hours again?"

Aidan scowled. Reaching Jackson's table—his table, damn it—Aidan cleared away a copy of the Miami *Herald* and crashed into a chair. "Federal business. Nothing you'd be interested in."

"Rumor has it you're the go-to guy on the Melvin

Baxter case. You making any headway?'' Jackson flipped out his napkin and laid it across his perfect pleats.

Aidan jammed his napkin into the collar of his shirt, not liking the direction of the conversation one bit. The last thing he needed in the Baxter case was attention from an attorney with political ambitions. Especially when that attorney also happened to be from a politically connected family the media loved to buzz about. ''I trust it matters a whole hell of a lot to you that you're bugging me about this at sunrise?''

''If you sew up your case soon, I can help prosecute it before election time. I realize this is kind of last-minute, but I'm under some pressure to throw in my hat for a state legislator bid.''

''Way to lay on the pressure, Jack. In other words, you want me to hurry up so you can make a few headlines just in time for a campaign.'' Aidan waved to his usual waitress. She was a breezy brunette who knew his regular order and liked to talk, but Aidan couldn't work up any enthusiasm for their normal flirtation routine this morning. Brianne's scent still clung to his clothes, his skin. Hell, even ten blocks away he couldn't escape her.

Jack held up his hands, all innocence. ''No pressure from me. I'm sure you've got enough raining down on you from the Bureau considering this is the most important case in the city right now.'' He gulped his coffee and gave Aidan a steady look. ''How you holding up?''

''Fine until some do-good politician comes along to pump up this investigation into a damn election issue.''

Aidan stepped over to the waitress's stand just outside the front door to the restaurant. He snagged a clean cup from the cart, poured himself coffee then sat back down. Obviously, the brunette was annoyed at his rebuff this morning and had decided to make him wait.

This was shaping up to be a hell of a day.

"So forget I said anything about prosecuting the case." Jackson stared out at the orange band of light low in the eastern sky that marked the sunrise. Ocean Drive remained quiet, but here and there people whizzed by the restaurant on Roller Blades, or an occasional jogger ran past with a dog. "That doesn't account for why you look like hell."

"You didn't hunt me down at my favorite breakfast haunt at seven in the morning to tell me I look like hell." Damned if he'd let Jackson get off that easily. The guy had more ambition and drive than anyone he'd ever met. They'd both been in the criminal justice program at the University of Miami and had taken the knowledge in different directions. Aidan had forged a path that he hoped would keep the city safer while Jackson's politically minded parents had prepared him from the cradle to be a big-time attorney in the family practice. If Jackson had gone out of his way to nudge Aidan on the Baxter case, there must be plenty of political buzz afoot.

Once it became a political issue, the press was never far behind. Then before he knew what hit him, Aidan's superiors would receive an eight-by-ten glossy of him and Brianne tangling limbs on her desk.

Shit.

Jackson straightened his tie that was already precisely aligned. "Maybe I didn't come to tell you that you look like hell, but I didn't come to strong-arm you into making an arrest either. Sure it wouldn't hurt me, but mostly I thought you ought to know you're getting more attention on this than you probably realize."

He snorted even though he was grateful for the heads-up. If he let Jack know he was appreciative, his so-called friend would be guilting him into attending all kinds of fund-raising golf tournaments and assorted do-gooder/politician stuff. No thanks. Aidan had enough on his plate without kissing babies on the politician's circuit. "And I suppose I need to know this so I'll start making politically correct decisions or something?"

"Do with it what you want, but I thought you deserved to know. If you choose to be more P.C. in the future, that's your call. You have to admit you're not exactly a by-the-book kind of guy." Jack had hauled Aidan's butt out of more than a few sticky situations in college. Between his smooth-talking shtick and the suits and ties he had sported even then, Jack kept them out of trouble while Aidan made sure they occasionally found enough to have a good time.

Aidan turned his baseball cap from backward to forward. He might not be a by-the-book kind of guy, but he wasn't a crook. His world wasn't as black and white as Jack's but it worked for him. "I can play the game when the situation calls for it."

Jackson arched a brow. "And I suppose the front-facing hat indicates you mean business now?"

"Damn straight it does."

Tossing a handful of bills on the table, Jackson rose.

"Then my work here is done. You're on the straight and narrow—or at least I've warned you that you ought to be. I need to get to the office for a meeting. Good luck digging up Baxter."

Aidan toasted his departure with his coffee cup, grateful to have his table to himself. After the way Brianne had tossed him out on his butt, he needed room to brood, damn it.

Jackson hovered by the door of his Mercedes convertible parked squarely in front of the restaurant, the car as sleek and squeaky-clean as its owner. "I hear you're spending a lot of time at Club Paradise now," he called back. "Word is they've got a hell of a floor show."

Aidan yawned and stretched. "It's a tough job but somebody's got to do it. You ought to drop by the club when you're done worrying about your damn public image. The women are gorgeous." Although the scantily clad, feathered showgirls couldn't compare to Brianne.

"I hear the owners are something of a sight to see too." Jackson slid into the driver's seat with a grin that was too damn happy for Aidan's taste. "I'll definitely be over there to check it out soon."

Aidan would have warned him to stay the hell away from one owner in particular, but Jackson was already maneuvering into traffic.

Not that he was worried his friend would turn Brianne's head. Okay, actually he was pretty sure a guy like Jackson would turn her head. But Aidan wasn't worried about it because he didn't have anything invested in his relationship with Brianne.

Last night had been a minor setback according to her. He wasn't about to let it mean more than that to him.

Assuming, of course, it didn't already.

As THE SUN SET, Brianne yawned and scribbled out yet another sentence in her revised security plan for the club. She was tired and edgy at the same time, exhausted from lack of rest yet thinking about Aidan and wondering how she'd handle sitting by his side tonight.

She had given up on sleep by noon today. After Aidan left she'd driven up to Palm Beach to the house she was renting in her mother's neighborhood. She'd only taken the home so she could keep an eye on Pauline who was between husbands and starting to fracture at the seams. The location certainly wasn't convenient.

But she'd awakened every hour engaged in erotic dreams of Aidan, so it wasn't as if she was getting much rest anyway. She'd made the drive back to South Beach to tweak a few flukes in her security system, but she'd already been sitting at a table overlooking the beach for hours and she only had a few pages filled with scattered notes about the changes she needed to make.

Pathetic.

She had to get her mind off Aidan. Maybe she needed to hire somebody to watch the security monitors for her until he finished up his investigation.

Not that she had much in her bank account after dumping her life savings into rescuing the club. She'd be lucky if she could afford to pay minimum wages to anyone for more than a day.

Scheming her way around the gorgeous, frustrating problem of Aidan Maddock, she tapped her pen on her gray legal pad until a feminine voice interrupted her thoughts.

"You look like you could use a drink." Summer stood behind her with two Good Fortune Potions in hand, cookies perched on the glasses. "Mind if I sit down?"

"You come bearing gifts. How can I refuse?" She nudged the chair opposite hers with the toe of her shoe to push it away from the table. She couldn't be rude even though she had a sneaking suspicion Summer would ask her all those probing, girl-talk sorts of questions Brianne never knew how to answer.

The upside of having worked in a male-dominated field for the last six years was that she could hold her own at the dartboard and the negotiating table. The downside was that she hadn't found the time or inclination to form many female friendships.

And judging from the intimate, personal things women sometimes liked to ask—at least, in Brianne's opinion they were personal, intimate things—she wasn't entirely sure she was ready to form female friendships. But maybe talking to Summer would offer her a distraction until she could get her head together enough to resist the temptation of Aidan tonight.

Summer set the glasses down and took a seat. Her gauzy turquoise dress was handkerchief-cut, with lots of peekaboo layers and a few high slits to show off her thighs. A yellow pendant in the shape of a star hung from her neck. She looked like Stevie Nicks in her gypsy period, but with a more cartoonish, graphic edge.

Summer had a visual appeal and immediate sense of style that would transfer well to camera. Brianne just wasn't sure how to relate to her in the real world.

"I was trying out a few fabric swatches in the Sweethearts Suite when I spied you out the window a few hours ago," Summer explained in between sips of her drink. "I was surprised just now when I brought some samples down to Lainie to see you still sitting out here. Is everything okay?"

No. Actually, everything sucked. She'd made a huge mistake by giving in to the raw sexual tug she felt between her and Aidan. Then she'd made things worse by offending him. And now she had to sit next to him all night—again—and pretend everything was business as usual.

Of course, she wasn't about to tell Summer she'd slept with the man who wanted to investigate criminal activity in their club. If they'd written a human resources handbook for on-the-job behavior, sleeping with FBI agents would probably be on the "don't" list.

"I'm sort of grappling with an ancient history issue I have going with Aidan Maddock," she surprised herself by saying. Of course, she hadn't admitted to having sex with him on top of her desk at closing time. But it was more than she'd intended to say. "I was pretty attracted to him the last time he investigated my ex-stepfather and it's been tripping me up a little bit when I have to sit next to him all night."

She gulped her drink after what felt like a huge confession. She needed fortitude of some kind before she started spilling her whole life history.

Summer failed to look surprised. "I had the feeling there was a romantic issue involved. I saw shades of pink in your aura and that's the impression I had right away."

Brianne suspected Summer merely had seen her bathed in the glow of the sunset, but she politely said nothing.

"I can run inside and dig out my tarot cards. Maybe there'll be an answer—"

Holding up both hands, she warded away *that* idea. "No, thank you. I think I'm too much of a nonbeliever for that to work." Too much of a scientific, mechanical mind. She liked to know how and why things added up.

Which was probably why she couldn't seem to get past her attraction to Aidan. It definitely didn't add up.

"Then do you mind if I offer you a little old-fashioned woman to woman advice?" She leaned closer, her yellow star pendant clanging against the table.

What did she have to lose? Brianne nodded.

"Don't fight it so hard. See what happens. Roll with it. That's the whole mentality of South Beach, and I swear you can't be happy in this city until you adopt its mantra as your own. Who needs to be uptight and rigid when you're lounging by the ocean?" She clinked her glass to Brianne's. "Live a little."

Not exactly the wisdom of the sages, but it resonated for Brianne. Worked for this moment and this problem.

And for some reason, she felt better. Lifting her glass, she drank to the notion. "Thank you. And I'll try."

In fact, maybe she just needed to turn her attention to new projects and a new direction. Commit herself to staying away from shady, dangerous men who couldn't follow a rule to save their lives.

She gazed out at the boats on the water and realized it was fully dark now. "I just hope I can leave Aidan in the past where he belongs."

She waited for Summer to say something, and when all remained silent in her friend's chair, Brianne wrenched her gaze from the bobbing lights on the water. Summer stared over Brianne's shoulder toward the club.

Turning, Brianne saw a familiar too-large silhouette standing on the patio that would be converted to a restaurant when the club was running at full steam.

A familiar, muscle-bound silhouette that had invaded her dreams and even now made her pulse pick up speed.

Damn.

"Don't hold your breath, girlfriend," Summer whispered across the table. "But I don't think that man is interested in your past. Psychic powers are not my cosmic forte but I'm still getting a strong vibe he's interested lock, stock and barrel in your here and now."

7

BY THE LIGHT OF a few flickering torches around the patio perimeter, Aidan thought he saw a flash of heat in Brianne's eyes. A second of unadulterated hunger that he recognized because he felt the same damn thing so keenly he hadn't slept more than a couple of hours that morning.

As Brianne straightened her spine and sauntered toward him with a long-stemmed glass in one hand, however, Aidan quickly realized he must have imagined that sizzling flash of connection between them. Brianne had mastered the art of cool detachment in her years as a New Yorker and she was giving him attitude with both guns. Blinking his gritty eyes, Aidan realized lack of sleep was screwing with his perceptions.

Not a good thing for a guy in his field.

He needed to get his mind off Brianne and back on his case. A feat which shouldn't be so freaking hard considering he had new evidence in hand, damn it.

Brianne glided to a stop a few feet away on the patio overlooking the ocean. Her friend—the part-owner with the crazy fashion sense and the off-key soprano—lingered down by the water, stretching her arms toward the stars like some kind of pagan priestess or maybe a yoga instructor. The woman was a trip.

And although Aidan's highly functional male eye recognized the blonde as a beauty, she didn't flick his switch the way Brianne could in her austere gray, ankle-length dress and bare feet.

The woman personified temptation.

She held out her half-full glass in offering—Eve with an apple. "You look like you need this more than me. Rough night, Agent Maddock?"

"I never indulge myself while I'm on the clock, Bri. But talk to me after hours and you can bet I'll be happy to take whatever you have to offer." If she planned to drive him to the brink of insanity with her in-your-face attitude, Aidan would damn well push a few boundaries, too.

He couldn't tell if he'd managed to rile her or not, however. She simply retracted the glass and took a long swallow of whatever it contained.

Aidan watched as her dark pink lips pursed around the rim of the goblet and she tossed her head back to sip the ruby-colored brew. His throat constricted along with hers as she drank.

And he was suddenly so damn thirsty he couldn't stand it.

She polished off the libation with a satisfied smack of her lips. "It was a one-time offer, Aidan. Guess you'll have to find your indulgences elsewhere tonight." Flicking open the tiny remote computer she wore strapped to her wrist like an oversized watch, Brianne pushed a few buttons. "I notice you're here early. You're welcome to my office if you'd like to start viewing the monitors, but I don't plan to join you until the club opens at eleven."

Seizing her hand, Aidan told himself he only touched her because he wanted to check out her latest gadgetry and not because he wanted to see if she still felt hot to the touch even when she operated in ice-queen mode.

"What's this?" He caught sight of a miniature monitor on the display screen before she snagged her wrist back.

And sure enough, her touch had been just as scorching as he'd remembered.

"It's a scaled-down version of the video screens in my office. I can't move the camera angles from here, but I can check out a handful of rooms from a stationary position."

Impressive. But the fact that she had so much security in place set up a few red flags, too. "You really need that much protection for the club, Bri?"

He didn't suspect her of being Melvin's accomplice. Was he being naive to rule her out when she had the technological skills—and the smarts—to funnel information to her former stepfather?

For a moment, her trademark bravado slipped a notch. And Aidan would have banked his paycheck on the fact that she wanted to confess something. But then she looked away, trailing an idle finger along the cast-iron patio table, and when she met his gaze again, her armor was right back in place.

This time, Aidan was positive it hadn't been his gritty eyes playing tricks on him.

"I'd rather have too much protection than not enough." She said it with enough vehemence that Aidan believed that much was true. Even the best of liars couldn't cultivate that kind of passion about something they didn't believe in.

Staring out at the water, Brianne took a deep breath as if to calm herself. "Besides, despite whatever you think about my connection to Mel Baxter, I have my own reasons for not wanting him to sneak past my guard. I don't want him around the club any more than you do."

"You're wrong there." He watched as the sea breeze caught a strand of her auburn hair and blew it across her cheek. He had all he could do not to hook his finger around that red lock and smooth it into place. He could almost feel the silky strand between his fingers. "The sooner Mel shows up here, the quicker I can leave you to run your business."

And the quicker he'd be able to put enough distance between them to assure himself he wouldn't touch her again.

"He's got no reason to come here." Brianne's brow furrowed, and Aidan had the impression she'd told herself as much more than once. "He has no connection to me or my mother anymore."

"Not true." There was no sense hiding his recent discovery from her. He wanted to ask her a few questions about it anyway.

"What do you mean?" Her green eyes narrowed.

"Mel might not be maintaining ties to you, but I'm guessing I've unearthed a very big connection to your mother. Do you know anything about a bank account under the name of Pauline Baxter with a balance of 1.2 million dollars that's been untouched for the last twelve years?"

Her mouth fell open. Wide. He had all the answer he needed.

Her jaw snapped shut as she recovered herself. She cleared her throat, tossed her hair over one shoulder. "My mother doesn't necessarily keep me informed of her financial status. She would have set that account up when I was little more a child."

Leaning on the wooden rail that surrounded part of the deck overlooking the ocean, Aidan wouldn't quibble with her on that note. Even though she would have been sixteen at the time, and by the age of eighteen, Brianne couldn't tell him often enough that she was all woman.

Not that his memories of Brianne's precocious sensuality had any bearing on his case.

"Do you have any reason to believe that money might not really belong to your mother?" He didn't necessarily expect her to be straight with him. She didn't trust him any more than he trusted her. But he asked her so he could gauge her reactions. And maybe solicit help in talking to her mother. "Because if it's an account Mel set up for himself in her name I can guarantee you he'll be back for it."

He almost felt guilty when she paled.

No, damn it. He *did* feel guilty when she paled.

"I'm sure my mother would have had to sign paperwork to set up an account. Show her license or something. Can't you investigate that kind of thing?" She didn't bite her lip, but Aidan could tell she wanted to. She was worried about her mother and trying like hell not to let him know.

"Bankers are pretty tight with their records unless

you push them to the wall. And there's a chance if we do that, word will get back to Mel that we're aware of the account. I'd rather talk to your mother about it first before we set off any warning signals like that. For all I know, I could be barking up the wrong tree.'' But he wasn't. He sensed it in his gut earlier today when he'd first struck pay dirt, and he sensed it even more strongly now as he picked up panicked vibes from Brianne.

That account didn't belong to Pauline Wolcott-Baxter-and etc. It belonged to Melvin Baxter and he'd be coming back for it.

All Aidan had to do was sit back and wait.

"You think it will help to talk to my mom?" Brianne wasn't even looking at him. The sea-scented breeze drifted by her, lifting strands of red hair to flutter around her neck. She stared down into her glass as she twirled the stem of the empty goblet in her hand—round and round in one direction. Round and round in the other.

"I think we'll find Melvin a hell of a lot faster if we do." He waited and watched her as nightlife took over the beach behind the resort. Couples strolled the sand in the moonlight while at a neighboring hotel, a few partiers sat around a bonfire and sang too loudly. Waves rolled over the shore in the background, the soft lull nearly lost in the steady growl of traffic from Ocean Drive.

He willed her to say yes. Needed her to agree.

Her cooperation was important to his case, but it was suddenly even more important to him personally and he wasn't quite sure why.

"I want to go with you when you talk to her." She quit twirling her glass and looked him in the eye.

Brianne had cooperated, but she was already issuing demands. Surprise, surprise.

Luckily, it just so happened he wanted her there with him anyway. Melvin's ex-wife might be more forthcoming with him if her daughter was around.

"Fine. But I can't afford to wait on this." How many more nights could he sit at the club shoulder-to-shoulder with Brianne before he forgot all about being a minor setback in her life and used any seductive means necessary to coerce her into another desktop encounter?

"It's a little late to show up on her doorstep tonight, don't you think?" She checked her computer screen again, making Aidan realize they'd been talking longer than he'd planned.

And making his agent instincts sit up and take notice again. Was she that committed to her job, or did Brianne have reason to watch her back?

Aidan made a mental note to find out. If she was hiding something that had any bearing on his case, he had no choice but to unearth it. And if she watched her back so thoroughly because she was scared of something—or someone—he'd pull every string at his disposal to make it disappear. "Tomorrow is soon enough. How about I pick you up at noon?"

Flipping shut the tiny door that covered her wristwatch computer gadget, Brianne nodded. "You're on. Let's head inside and I'll write my address down for you." She took a few steps and then stopped. Pivoted.

Stared him down. "Then again, you probably already know where I live, don't you?"

"They don't hand out the badges to any sucker on the street, Bri. I did learn a thing or two about investigative work to get where I am today." He refused to apologize for doing his job well. If she didn't like the lack of privacy, that was her problem.

"I just hope you remember who it is you're investigating." She whirled around to continue on her way to her office, ankle-length skirt churning around her feet with her purposeful walk.

Aidan followed the path of those sexy bare feet, telling himself he knew exactly who he was after in this case.

And he had Brianne in his sights for a different reason entirely.

BRIANNE WAS NOT HAPPY to wake up alone the next morning.

She'd been a good girl and followed sound logic in staying away from Aidan the night before. In an effort to put some distance between them, she'd found every reason in the world to venture into the club to monitor activity with her own eyes while leaving Aidan in her office. She couldn't be next to him for two minutes without wanting him and she couldn't be next to him for five minutes without a restless ache creeping up her thighs and making her so edgy she couldn't sit still.

So she'd spent most of the night roaming the corridors of Club Paradise and feeling Aidan's eyes on her from the other side of the video cameras around every corner.

Now, rubbing her eyes shortly before noon in her oversize sleigh bed—the only piece of furniture she owned that wasn't sleekly modern—she wondered what had ever made her decide to be a good girl in regard to Aidan. Being bad was so much more rewarding, damn it. Her shower was frustrating because she wanted Aidan's hands on her wet body. Her orange juice annoyed her because she wanted to taste Aidan's lips.

She paced the espresso-colored carpet of the small contemporary house she was renting in Palm Beach, searching for a distraction and thinking she'd have to retrieve a few more of her gadgets from storage now that she was pretty well moved in. She had her programmable menu on her refrigerator, and the house came with a nifty chandelier-lowering switch for the huge light fixture in the hallway, but other than that, she had nothing to play with in her spare time.

Her restless, keyed-up and horny-as-hell spare time.

Damn Aidan Maddock for giving her way too much sensual material for her fantasies.

Flicking the shiny chrome chandelier up and down, Brianne decided she should make a master remote for the house so she could control everything from her wrist computer. And she also needed to beef up her security systems. Her experience with a boyfriend gone rogue in New York had taught her the value of efficient security. Now, she stared up at the clock and wondered why she'd agreed to spend her one and only night off in Aidan's company. The club was closed Mondays, yet she would be with him again today for who knows how long.

Spying a leather portfolio on the bench beside her front door, Brianne remembered Summer asking her to look at the new design plan for the revamped Sweethearts Suite. Seizing upon something—anything—to take her mind off steamy thoughts of Aidan, Brianne cracked open the buttery black case and dropped on to the bench seat to have a look at what Summer had come up with.

Burgundy velvet spilled out on to her lap, followed by a long swatch of deep red satin and a thick strip of black silk. The portfolio was stuffed full with pictures torn from catalogs and sketches Summer had made. At the top of the left-hand page, she'd scrawled Bad-Girl Bordello and had roughed out a drawing of the proposed room.

The burgundy velvet would drape the bed. The dark red satin would be shirred and gathered on the walls. Black silk would trim the bed drapes, the lampshades and the bed skirt. The room would be wildly decadent and immediately sensual.

Brianne loved the concept on sight even as the restless ache for Aidan kicked up another heated degree. Or five. She could see Aidan lying in that darkly sensual bed. Waiting for her.

She flipped the page, unwilling to let velvet visions draw her more deeply into provocative imaginings. Right now she wanted to work, not engage in more erotic fantasies about Aidan.

Of course, the next page was overflowing with ornate gilt mirrors. Mirrors that reminded her of the night she'd played out her long-standing strip search fantasy with Aidan in her office.

Not good.

Turning another page, she found carved stonework figures to decorate the mantle. Little statues in the shape of—she squinted a closer look at the picture— sexual anatomy. Breasts covered by broad, masculine hands. Feminine thighs splayed. A penis of astounding proportion beside it.

Brianne cursed the sexy new bordello design and the fever that seemed to be crawling over her skin. Flushed and edgy, she thrust aside the portfolio.

Just as the doorbell rang.

Oh. No.

She sat there frozen two feet from the front door. Why hadn't she heard him pull in the driveway? Because she was too caught up in pictures of erect penises, that's why.

Before she could get her head together and her temperature under control, a shadow blocked the sun through the narrow sidelight beside her door. Aidan's face hovered in the frosty glass, no doubt spying her there.

Flustered, she jumped up to answer the door. Better to be overheated than have him think for a minute she was nervous. She wasn't an eighteen-year-old with a crush on him anymore.

Taking deep breaths she headed toward the door and pulled it open. Aidan waited on her front step wearing a gray suit and tie, his backward baseball cap nowhere in sight.

He cleaned up well—she had to grant him that much. His hair was still too long, and he still sported the Fu Manchu beard and mustache combo that made him look a little too dangerous to be on the right side of the law, but otherwise he resembled an FBI agent for once.

And he managed to be sexy as hell at the same time.

He pulled open her screen door and eyed her with heated familiarity. "Red's your color, Bri. I give it two thumbs up."

She struggled to make sense of his words until she followed his gaze down to her midsection where she still clutched the burgundy velvet, the dark red satin and the black silk.

The sight of those fabrics made her pulse rev double time. The plush material between her fingers brought back distinct memories of what she'd been thinking about doing with Aidan and the velvet two minutes before he'd arrived.

She dropped them on the bench, sensing the heat climb her cheeks. Not that she was embarrassed, damn it. Just a little more turned on than she cared to admit. "I was just going over some decorating samples—" She was talking too fast, her words breathless and rushed. Slipping into her shoes, she told herself to slow down. Relax. Summer's advice to "roll with it" flitted through her brain. "The Sweethearts Suite needs to be updated."

Aidan edged his way inside, even though she'd meant to run out the door before he had the chance to come in today. The last thing she needed was any sort of privacy—intimacy—with this man.

"What are you updating it into?" Aidan stepped around her to take a closer look at the material. "A brothel?"

"Summer's calling it the Bad-Girl Bordello, but I'm not sure we'll keep the name." She held her chin high, struggled for the cool distance she'd managed with him just a few days ago. Where the hell had it disappeared? Probably went up in flames along with her common sense the night she played sexy games with Aidan.

Now, she watched his fingers slide over the soft length of the rich fabrics and suppressed a shiver of pure hunger.

The motion of his hands mesmerized her until the foyer seemed to shrink and the scent of Aidan's after-shave became a heady aphrodisiac.

"Are these the room designs?" He reached for the open portfolio alongside the bench, perhaps drawn by the sketches and the colored photos taped beside them.

Colored photos of penis statuary.

Brianne scrambled for the book as Aidan let out a whistle. "Good God, woman, what kind of joint are you ladies running over there?"

She reached for the portfolio, but Aidan was totally engrossed in the subject matter now and he held on tight to the leather case as he sank down on to the bench in her hallway.

"Aidan." She strove for a matter-of-fact tone of voice, but she half wondered how the erotic artwork would affect him.

Was it wishful thinking, or did she notice him gulp a few times?

Brianne backed up a step, not wanting to be anywhere near the man while they both were thinking sexy thoughts. They'd be sprawled across the foyer floor in no time, making yet another huge mistake of judgment.

The phone rang while she observed him. A fortuitous distraction?

She hurried to the kitchen, skirting around a high-tech cooking station that was totally wasted with her non-existent culinary skills to grab the phone. Maybe it was her mother finally returning her call.

"Hello?" Brianne answered.

And waited.

And waited.

"Hello?" There was no dial tone on the other end, but a rather distinct sense of someone there. Listening. Unease crept through her. "Hello?"

The phone clicked and the connection died, a dial tone taking the place of dead air.

A niggle of fear took the place of unease.

Irrational, misplaced fear, but there was fear nevertheless. Because no matter how many reasonable scenarios she could concoct for the three hang-ups she'd had in the last two days, she couldn't ignore her gut hunch that told her it wasn't coincidence.

On top of all her other problems this week and despite her best precautions, she had the feeling her psycho ex-boyfriend had located her.

And obviously, he wasn't trying to find her because he wanted to talk.

8

AIDAN'S AGENT INSTINCTS kicked in the second time Brianne said "hello." By the third, her voice hit a thready note that gave his libido a knockout punch and sent him into the kitchen to investigate.

She was just settling the receiver back in its cradle, her movements slow and deliberate. Careful. Her pale face matched the floor's pristine white tiles.

"Everything okay?" He reached out to steady her, his hand settling along her shoulder and the strap of her brown silk tank top. Two minutes ago he wouldn't let himself touch her for fear he wouldn't be able to stop. Now, something about her rigid posture made him think she needed to be touched. Reassured.

But damned if he knew why.

"Everything's fine." She gave him a phony-as-hell smile. Nodded with a jerky movement. "Shall we head over to my mother's?"

"What was that all about?" Her skin was cool beneath his hand. Chill bumps ran down her arm, giving him damn good reason to think she was nervous. Maybe even scared.

"Wrong number, I guess." She charged toward the door and back into the foyer, her heels tapping out a sure rhythm on the tile floor. With restless energy she picked up the length of burgundy velvet and proceeded to fold it into neat halves. "People can be so rude."

Aidan watched her fold the red satin next, her obsessive attention to smoothing out the wrinkles in the fabric confirming his suspicion she was hiding something. "Has Mel been in touch with you, Brianne?"

Her grip tightened on the satin, her clutched fist introducing a whole new round of wrinkles. "How many times do I have to answer that damn question, Aidan? No, he hasn't, as I believe I've told you more than once."

"If he's trying to blackmail you into helping him—"

"That is totally absurd." She tossed the satin in a heap on the bench. "And just what do you think anyone could ever blackmail me with? I might be helping Summer with the Bad-Girl Bordello, but despite what you'd like to think, I'm not that much of a bad girl. I resent that you continually insist on suggesting otherwise."

Frustration fired through him. "Maybe I wouldn't have to think otherwise if you'd ever be straight with me. I'd bet the Harley that you're hiding something from me right now, and I'd bet my retirement fund that it has something to do with that phone call you just received. If you're not willing to share a damn thing with me, then I have no choice but to think you're guilty of something."

The comment put the color back in her cheeks in no time. She looked ready to throttle him. "Has it ever occurred to you I might have a life apart from you and my former stepfather? That I don't want to tell you about that phone call because it doesn't have a damn thing to do with your case and it's none of your business?''

Wrenching a set of keys off a series of hooks by the front door, Brianne yanked her purse off the coat tree. ''And for that matter, the only reason you're in my house today is because I agreed to help you out with this infernal investigation of yours. So in light of my generosity in this, the least you could do is stay out of my private affairs.''

He watched her tug open the front door while she glared back at him, steam practically hissing from her ears. Couldn't she see he was only trying to help?

Blasted independent woman.

''Fine. If you choose to handle your private *affairs* by yourself, even though something has you scared, I can't force you to share it with me. But don't be surprised if I'm watching you twice as often.'' He stepped closer, near enough to catch a hint of the perfume that had driven him crazy the other night. Memories of Brianne's naked body wrapped around his came screaming back to taunt him. ''And don't be surprised to find me three steps behind you, watching your back.''

Watching *you.*

He thought it so strongly, he was convinced she heard it. Her grip tightened around the doorknob.

''You've got a job to do and I understand that.'' She shrugged. ''You do what you have to.''

He didn't just have to. When it came to watching Brianne, he *wanted* to. Hell, he couldn't take his eyes off her most of the time anyway.

Her heels clicked down the sidewalk, leaving him to lock the door behind him. Then again, knowing Brianne, she probably had a gadget of some sort that would lock the door from afar. Aidan clicked the lock into place manually anyway, taking one last longing look at the burgundy velvet folded on the bench seat as he did.

He'd wanted to wrap her up in that lush fabric the minute she'd answered the door with it clutched in her hands. He'd entertained brief visions of them rolling around the foyer floor before they went to her mother's house, but he couldn't afford to spend time on seduction now.

Not that Brianne would have necessarily allowed herself to be seduced in the first place.

Damn.

He pulled the door closed behind him and stomped his way down to his car in the relentless late-summer sunshine, frustrated on more levels than he could count. Ducking under the low-hanging branches of a squat palm tree at the end of the walkway, he told himself he needed to get his priorities straight soon— like yesterday, maybe—before he blew this case all over again.

"I appreciate you helping me secure an audience with your mother, Brianne. I know you probably had better things to do today than give me a hand, but thank you." He opened the passenger door for her and swiped a baseball cap off the front seat of his car, determined to get his head on straight.

Therefore, he did *not* watch the way her black silky

pants clung to the curve of her hips as she eased her way in.

Shutting the door behind her as soon as she stepped inside, Aidan didn't give her time to respond. Instead, he went around to his side of the car and slid into the driver's seat. "Keeping this case out of the media spotlight means a hell of a lot to me, so the more low-key the investigation, the better. If Mel doesn't know how much manpower we're investing to find him, he's more likely to be drawn out of hiding sooner." He shifted the car into reverse. "And I'll be waiting for him."

Brianne was silent for a moment as they sat in stop-and-go traffic surrounded by landscaped sidewalks and intermittent palm trees groomed to the exact same height. The houses turned from big to palatial as they made the short drive from Brianne's house to her mother's.

Instead of swing sets in the backyard, the Palm Beach crowd was more likely to have swimming pools surrounded by gargantuan-screened cages or private tennis courts. Jackson would feel at home here maybe, but the ritzy streets bore little resemblance to Aidan's upbringing in downtown Miami.

Finally, she turned to him, her perfume teasing his nose. "Why is it so important to you to bring in Mel? You can't be this obsessive about all your cases. What makes Melvin Baxter such a prize catch for you?"

"I don't know who told you I wasn't obsessive about all my cases, but it's a lie. Injustice pisses me off and I like catching crooks. It's gratifying as hell to lock up bad guys." He turned on to her mother's street, just a few blocks from Brianne's.

If they lived that close together, they were probably on good terms now, even though Aidan remembered their relationship had been tense ten years ago. Would Brianne have called Pauline to warn her not to say anything to him today? It was a chance he was prepared to take in order to corner Mel's ex-wife for a few minutes. And he had every intention of keeping an eye out for any telling looks between mother and daughter.

"But I have to admit I'm pretty gung ho to lock up Mel because he slipped away the first time around. There's a pride issue at stake here." Maybe a dumb-ass reason, but it was at least partially the truth. He wasn't about to go into the details of Melvin swindling his grandparents or the inter-agency cover-ups that had ensured he'd flub the Baxter investigation. He didn't have enough hard evidence to prove all the collusion that went on anyway. At least not yet. "That first case was the only one I ever screwed up, so I'm working to redeem myself."

His conscience had bothered him for ten years over the whole debacle. But he'd lost the most sleep over knowing his best friend's father had been the primary force behind the effort to bury his case against Melvin.

"You didn't screw up anything. I followed the papers from New York and even the *Herald* suggested there was no trail to follow. You can't gather evidence that isn't there." She took out a tiny silver mirror from her purse and checked out her reflection. The gesture was totally at odds with everything he knew about her, probably brought on by their proximity to her mother's house.

She surprised him even more when she took out a tiny pair of black-rimmed glasses and shoved them on her nose.

Very curious.

"Everything went wrong on that damn case from the word go. I didn't expect Mel to be so slick from his profile, and that was my biggest mistake. You can be damn sure I never underestimated a suspect again." Aidan had found out later he'd been put in a position to fail because Jackson's father had invested in Mel's long-ago crooked enterprise and hadn't wanted the connection uncovered.

Why else would he have been given bogus leads and a screw-up partner? Sooner or later Aidan would need help uncovering the corruption in the agency. And, painful though it might be, Jackson Taggart was probably the most logical guy to help him root it out.

After Aidan had Melvin behind bars.

Brianne cleared her throat. "And you didn't expect the crook's stepdaughter to hit on you, right? Sorry I didn't stay out of your way back then. I know I caused you some major grief."

More guilt than grief.

He'd felt like a heel for even listening to her barrage of erotic proposals given her age at the time. Five years difference seemed like a lifetime when the woman in question was eighteen and on her way to college while he was already independent and ready to tackle the world as an agent.

Pulling into her mother's driveway, he took quick note of the three-story brick colonial home with fat white columns lining the front facade, then peered across the front seat. "You don't have a thing to be sorry for, Bri. It was me who messed up the investigation. You were just…" Distracting the hell out of him to thwart his case against her stepfather? No. He didn't believe that anymore. "…something of a firecracker. And I'd be lying if I said the come-ons didn't flatter me."

She blinked back at him behind her glasses. Surprised.

And that was enough confession time for him today, thank you very much. Time to get down to business before he got caught up in Brianne all over again.

"I'll follow your lead with Pauline. You ready to go?" He was out of the car before she could answer, eager to put the conversation back on firmer footing. Comfortable footing.

Work, he could deal with. He'd kick ass on this investigation like he had every other one since that fateful first time out.

No way in hell would he get tripped up by a woman again. First Brianne. Then his ex-wife. He'd learned a few lessons since then, damn it, and he knew he couldn't concentrate on work and a woman at the same time.

And work was far easier to figure out.

He opened Brianne's door and watched her exit the blue Ford with the regal grace of a movie star hitting the red carpet. Any trace of insecurity he'd glimpsed on their way over was now hidden by her studious-looking glasses and plastered behind a cool veneer.

Interesting.

"She's fragile," Brianne informed him as she

pressed the doorbell. "And there's no telling how she'll respond to questions about Mel. I told her not to panic, but I don't know how she'll—"

The door swung wide to reveal a gently rounded woman in her early fifties, her brown hair knotted behind her head, her legs encased in black tights and her body outfitted in a red satin dress printed with orange and green flowers. She looked a bit like a Chinese lantern, a bright spot of color framed in the stucco doorway of her Palm Beach home.

"Welcome, Brianne darling. Won't you and your friend come in?" She smiled and gestured them in with the practiced moves of a lifetime hostess. Aidan had her pegged for a garden club president or maybe a Junior Leaguer.

He itched to get past the introductions and start with the questions, but he was letting Brianne take the lead. As he followed her and her mother into a powder-blue parlor complete with elaborate silver tea service—the pot already steaming—he had the feeling he'd be itching for quite a while.

BRIANNE COULD ALMOST HEAR Aidan's inward groan when they stepped into her mother's fussy parlor with the profusion of fresh flowers and the scented candles lit along the sideboard. Any minute Pauline would be rolling out the lemon drops and asking what they thought of the upcoming local elections.

Not that she truly enjoyed politics.

But it was on Pauline's list of polite "company" talk that she'd been trotting out for guests Brianne's whole life. Welcome to Uptight Women's Anonymous.

"Mom, we won't take up your whole afternoon. We just wanted to ask you a few questions about Mel. This is—"

"Honestly, Brianne, you just walked in the door. Tell me all about your new job. And you must introduce me to your gentleman friend. Have a seat." She helpfully pointed to a spot on the overstuffed loveseat.

Brianne would frankly rather tangle with a whole club full of drunken and out-of-control patrons than subject herself to the perils of her mother's parlor small-talk, but ingrained habits were difficult to break. Especially when it came to mother-daughter relationships.

She sat.

Aidan lowered himself on to the cushion beside her even though the useless piece of furniture wasn't large enough for a cat much less two adults who didn't need to be plastered leg-to-leg. His presence was too close, too male, and oddly comforting at the same time.

"So Brianne, don't keep me in suspense any longer. Tell me who is this handsome young man with you?" Pauline's eyes roamed over Aidan with genuine interest. "He reminds me of my own Stewart, so tall and dark."

Brianne mustered a smile for the reference to her long-deceased father, the man Pauline had always compared all others against. Aidan was scoring high praise in her mother's book.

Apparently Mom hadn't made the connection that Aidan was only sitting on her loveseat in order to pry loose some more information about her ex-husband.

"Mom, this is Aidan Maddock. Maybe you remember him as the investigating agent the last time Melvin was in trouble?''

Pauline extended her hand. ''I can't say that I do. Of course that was a long time ago. It's a pleasure to meet you, Aidan.''

He nodded, shook her hand. Smiled in a way that charmed cigarette girls and society matrons alike. ''Likewise. I appreciate you talking to us today.''

Pauline practically beamed. ''I always enjoy visits from my daughter. She's lived far away from me for so many years that it's a pleasure to see her more often.'' She reached for the silver tea service, her hostess manners coming to the fore. ''Let me pour you a cup of tea while we talk and you can tell me all about how you and Brianne met.''

Aidan snagged a white-and-gold teacup off the cart and held it out to be filled. A definite protocol glitch, but one that just might speed them through this visit a little faster. ''That's one of my favorite stories. But I think Brianne tells it better than I do.'' He arched an expectant brow in her direction. ''Don't you, honey?''

Ignoring him and the quick burst of heat his sexy smile ignited over her skin, she took the teapot from her mother's hands and filled three cups in efficient succession. She didn't have the time or the inclination to play tea party today. Not when she had the weight of Aidan's gaze on her and the memory of her recent string of phone hang-ups preying upon her mind. She couldn't bear to think about who those calls might be from. ''Aidan is an FBI agent, not a personal friend, Mom. He needs to know if you've heard from Melvin lately.''

Pauline frowned. "You truly inherited your father's manners, Brianne. You're always in such a hurry."

Could she help it if she didn't like to waste time? The possible explanations for her phone hang-ups made her want to run home and implement a few new protective measures. She wasn't about to spend the afternoon pretending Aidan was her beau just to amuse Pauline.

"Sorry Mom. Aidan and I both need to get to work soon." She felt just a little twinge of guilt at the lie. But she devoted enough time to her mother since she'd returned to Florida between balancing Pauline's checkbook—a Herculean task in itself—and tackling her grocery shopping on a weekly basis so she'd at least have something mildly nutritious in the house besides Earl Grey and champagne. "Have you talked to Mel lately?"

Settling back on the settee with a sniff, Pauline maintained her perfect posture. "You know he hasn't called me since I married Ray. I think he took my fourth marriage rather badly, the poor man."

After Brianne's father died, Pauline had married a white-collar crook, a control-freak business executive and a wealthy playboy in quick succession, but she'd never managed to recapture the love that she'd found with Brianne's father.

While Pauline's lack of judgment in men annoyed Brianne, it also unnerved her a little to think she might have inherited the quality.

Aidan gulped back his tea and replaced the cup on the cart with a clang. "Do you remember if Melvin

Baxter ever asked you to open a bank account for him, Pauline?''

Brianne wondered how her mother would react to such a blunt question, but she was much more tolerant of candor from men.

She flashed a conspiratorial smile at Brianne. ''My husbands haven't typically let me anywhere near their banking affairs, Mr. Maddock. Ask my daughter what a failure I am at money matters.''

Aidan leaned forward, his weight shifting the seat cushion next to Brianne as his thigh grazed hers ever so slightly. She had a momentary vision of their limbs entwined and the hard heat of his thighs pressed against hers that night on top of her desk.

She edged closer to the other side of the loveseat to increase the distance between them, but the liquid heat remained in her legs.

''It's an important question, ma'am. Do you have any bank records dating from the years you were married to Baxter that you can consult? I have reason to believe that a financial connection remains between the two of you.''

Brianne sensed the tension in Aidan from the taut set of his muscles beside her. Though his voice held a note of pleasant charm and gentle coaxing, she didn't miss the telltale urgency threading through his tone.

She desperately wanted her mother to deny any lingering association between herself and Melvin, but at the same time, her gut told her Pauline had to be ignorant of an account with over a million dollars languishing in her name for so many years.

Her mother's eyes widened. ''My daughter made me

turn over all my banking records to her last month when she insisted she balance my checkbook. Brianne, you are welcome to show this nice gentleman anything he wants to see in regard to my account information.''

Either her mom knew nothing about the account and her affiliation with a well-known criminal, or she was lying through her teeth.

Great. Just great.

While Pauline, hostess extraordinaire, deftly turned the conversation from her crook ex-husband to quiz Aidan about his favorite restaurants in town—a long-time staple question in her guest itinerary—Brianne brooded over the fact that her mother might be in a lot of trouble.

Of course, trouble was nothing new to Pauline who'd wiggled in and out of tight scrapes with her string of loser husbands for years. What upset Brianne more was realizing that not only was her mother in over her head with Mel, but that she herself wasn't much better off if her recent rash of phone hang-ups were originating with her ex-boyfriend.

Strange to think she had far more in common with her mother than she'd ever suspected. No matter how well organized Brianne kept her checkbook or how coolly sterile she made her own gadget-happy household, she would still share one undeniable trait with her mother.

A bad habit of choosing men who were all wrong for them—and also potentially dangerous.

Snitching a macaroon off the tiered cake stand full of candies on the teacart, Brianne gave a momentary ear to the conversation at hand and discovered Pauline knee-deep in discussing politics with Aidan. That could keep them going for another fifteen minutes, and it might save Brianne from having to tell her mother all about the club's first week in business. She munched the macaroon and wondered idly how she and her mom could have gotten so mixed up with their choices in men.

Even if she discounted the creepy boyfriend in college who'd bummed money off her at every turn and finally made off with her ATM card for an unauthorized shopping spree, she still couldn't deny her involvement with Jimmy had been scary in the end.

She'd met him while he was playing in a blues café one night and had thought him incredibly sensitive and romantic. Too soon he'd turned oversensitive and prone to depression when he'd been certain she'd been out with other men any time she left her apartment.

When she'd tried to break off their relationship, he'd taken to following her—never hurting her, but the threat had been there. He'd creeped her out, turned her into a homebody when she'd always been outgoing. She'd jumped all over the chance to return to Florida and invest in Club Paradise.

What continued to haunt her about the whole Jimmy experience was that all the signs of possessiveness and dark moodiness had been there from the beginning, but Brianne had chosen to ignore them.

Brushing the crumbs from her macaroon off her mouth and on to a linen napkin, she had to ask herself why she still didn't know better than to involve herself with dangerous men.

Now she'd been in Florida for all of a month and

already she'd caved to Aidan Maddock's charm. Sure, he was a far cry from a stalker, but he wore his penchant for danger on his sleeve between his FBI job, his tendency to skate around the rules and his open admiration for loose-lipped cigarette girls like Daisy.

How could she let herself get mixed up with a guy like that? Time to put some serious distance between her and Aidan, starting today.

She didn't need a man in her life right now, but if she ever decided to venture into a relationship, she would definitely find some nice, upstanding guy who wouldn't drag her into his FBI cases.

Of course, there could be a downside to that scenario. A nice, upstanding guy might not be as apt to play strip search games guaranteed to drive her wild.

But that was a risk she was going to have to take.

9

AIDAN TAPPED OUT A TUNE on the steering wheel as he drove Brianne home through the tree-lined streets of ritzy Palm Beach. Restless energy consumed him, the simmering excitement that always came when he made solid progress on a case.

Pauline Wolcott-Baxter-Menendez-Simmons had been every bit as flighty and superficial as he'd remembered from his dealings with her the first time around—nothing like his own mother who possessed a tireless work ethic and never relied on anyone. He'd seen a new side of Brianne as she'd quietly collected Pauline's bills from a small desk on her way out of the house. How long had she been taking care of her mother? Moreover, he wondered if anyone had ever truly taken care of Brianne.

As he slowed for a jogger running with a tiny white poodle, Aidan turned his thoughts back to his new information. Pauline didn't know about the account in her name. He guessed Melvin had set it up without her knowledge to help funnel his money and hide his criminal maneuverings. Brianne had told him flat-out that her mother had no record of the account in question.

Although, come to think of it, that was the *last* thing she had told him.

And she'd said it way back when they were walking out of her mother's house.

"You okay?" he asked as he pulled into the driveway of her low-slung contemporary home on a more modest street. "You're awfully quiet."

"I'm fine." She removed the fake glasses that she seemed to have worn solely for her mother's benefit and tucked a pair of sunglasses on her nose. "Thanks for the lift."

She was already shoving open the car door.

"Hey, wait a minute." He clicked off the ignition and scrambled his way out of the car to head her off before she got to the house and slammed the door in his face. "What gives? Did I screw up the tea drinking or something?"

She slowed her determined steps but her spine remained ramrod-straight. Unyielding. "I have no quibbles with your tea drinking. But I do have other business to attend this afternoon, Aidan. I guess I considered our work together done for the day."

"Damn it, Brianne, do you have to act so freaking frosty with me all the time?" It was no secret that when they got within five feet of one another they generated enough heat to melt polar ice caps.

Tilting her sunglasses downward, she peered at him over the rims. Her green eyes narrowed with cool assessment, but her cheeks flushed with just a little agitation.

Which was pretty damn gratifying to see for a change.

"I think some frost is in order between you and me, Aidan, if we don't want to end up crossing any more personal boundaries. Excuse me if I choose to spend my free time somewhere else besides glued to your side.'' She jammed the sunglasses back into place, but she didn't walk away.

Of course, she couldn't escape into her house since he blocked the front walkway.

He searched for a retort but got diverted in the image of her glued to his side.

Her disgruntled sigh saved him from the erotic torture of that particular picture. ''Do you mind? I have a lot of things to do today.''

''So do I, damn it.'' How could she rob him of the satisfaction he felt from making progress on his case so fast? ''If you'd quit distracting me, I'd be able to ask you a few more questions and we could both move on.''

''*I'm* distracting you?'' She crossed her arms, tilted her hip to one side. It was the pose of a skeptic, but the hip action in particular drew his eye.

''Hell yes, you're distracting me.'' His hands itched to realign her, to guide her hip back into place where he wouldn't be so apt to stare at it, but he knew damn well once he touched her there'd be no stopping.

Unless, of course, she slugged him for such a brazen act. An outcome that was entirely possible.

He closed his eyes and willed his thoughts to focus. ''Aidan—''

Luckily, without the visual of Brianne to preoccupy him, he remembered what he wanted. He opened his eyes, stared her down through the barrier of her dark glasses. ''Would you mind if I took your mother's banking records and copied them? I can bring everything back to you in an hour.''

"You realize this is above and beyond on my part?''

"I'll be out of your way the rest of the day. You don't even have to let me in the front door.'' In fact, far better that she didn't let him in the front door because if he got within ten feet of her design book full of sexy paintings and erotic statues, he'd never be able to keep his hands off her.

Her nod was clipped, forced. But it was a nod nevertheless.

Aidan counted that as a victory and stepped aside to allow her a clear path. Heaven knew after an encounter with her mother, she deserved a break today. Socialite Pauline Simmons seemed like a nice enough lady, but she probably had even less in common with her technically inclined daughter than he did.

And that was saying something.

He prepared to follow Brianne into the house—or rather, to the front steps—when he noticed she wasn't moving. She remained frozen on the sidewalk as she stared up at the front door.

And a huge arrangement of flowers lying on the welcome mat.

Who the hell had the nerve to send Brianne flowers when he'd been with her—intimately—just two nights ago?

Not that he would say as much. He had a little more couth than that. "Nice blooms. Are you breaking hearts again, Bri?''

When she didn't respond, he tore his eyes from the

obscenely large arrangement to look at her. She seemed unnaturally still.

"Bri?" He wished he could see behind those damn sunglasses of hers. Her cheeks looked pale but for two blotches of bright color in the middle.

Was she embarrassed? Somehow, that didn't fit with his image of her.

"It's nothing." She waved away the moment with a jumpy swat of her hand. "I'll just go grab those banking records and you can be on your way."

She hustled up the steps and sidestepped the flowers. No easy task considering their girth on the front mat. Dropping her keys once—make that twice—she finally managed to get the door open and disappeared inside.

And still she hadn't so much as glanced at the card on the gargantuan bouquet.

Obviously she knew exactly who had sent her the posies. Orchids, actually. Aidan recognized the assorted purple and white petals from his semifrequent trips to the florist during his short stint as a married man. Orchids had always been out of his price range, even when he'd spent seventy-two hours straight on the job and pissed off Natalie to the extreme.

This offering must have cost some guy an arm and a leg.

And just why should it bother him that Brianne had found a boyfriend with deep pockets? Good for her.

Ya-freaking-hoo.

He mentally scrambled for reasons why knowing who sent the damn flowers had any bearing on his case so he could feel justified in reading the card. Too bad he came up dry in an attack of principles.

Damn.

Brianne was back in a flash anyhow, shoving a manila envelope in his face, her dark sunglasses still barring her eyes from view. "Here you go. No need to bring them back today. I'll just pick up the package tomorrow when I see you at the club."

"Why do I feel like I'm being dismissed?"

"Damn it, Aidan, I'm not into playing Miss Manners like my mother. I helped you today—repeatedly—and I'm not about to feel guilty because I've got other things I need to take care of."

Like her high roller boyfriend.

Aidan felt a headache the size of Melvin Baxter's bankroll coming on. "Fine. I'm going to swing by the club this afternoon anyway to check things out. You want some help bringing the five-ton flower extravaganza inside before I go?"

She shook her head. Vehemently. "No thanks. I've got them." She stretched her lips into something that might have resembled a smile had there been any warmth of feeling behind it. "Bye, Aidan."

The door shut with a soft thud and a dull click of a lock on the other side.

Well, damn.

No denying it, he was a little miffed.

If Brianne had some other guy waiting in the wings, she shouldn't be playing out hot and sexy fantasies with him. And it was too damn late to tell himself to leave his emotions out of it.

Judging by how fast miffed turned into jealous as hell, Aidan couldn't deny his emotions were already too damn engaged.

But he wouldn't be helping his investigation if he went down that road. Sending Melvin Baxter to a federal penitentiary would offer him closure on his long-ago case from hell. He'd waited, kept silent about all the in-house cover-ups involved for too many years to botch up his chance for redemption now. He'd lift a blot from his name that had hovered around him no matter how much he'd kicked ass in every assignment since then.

Regardless of how enticing Brianne and her penchant for role-playing might be, his focus had to remain on his job.

BRIANNE REFUSED TO open the front door again until her hands stopped shaking. She watched, fixated, as her fingers trembled over the dead bolt.

The flowers still waited outside on the front step as Aidan's car rumbled out of the driveway.

Who'd have thought orchids wrapped in tissue paper and surrounded with exotic greenery could scare her to the roots of her hair?

They had to be from Jimmy. There hadn't been any other man in her life for over a year, except Aidan. And *he* obviously hadn't sent them.

When she'd first spied the bouquet on her doorstep, she'd wanted nothing more than to jump behind him and make him go read the card. His whole job was about protecting people—surely he could help her figure out how to shake one nightmare of an ex-boyfriend?

But then again, why dump on him after she'd already promised she would stay out of his way in this investigation? She'd distracted him during his first case against Mel, why divert him from his cause all over again?

No, Aidan didn't need to hear about her problems. It was enough that he'd been there to walk her to the door and make sure no one jumped out from the bushes. She'd call the local cops in a minute.

Perfectly rational, right? Okay, maybe not super rational given that her stupid pride had also been driving her actions. What would he think of her if he discovered she was not only linked to a big-time swindler in Miami, but a potentially dangerous stalker in New York? She was obviously quite skilled at associating herself with scary guys.

Gulping a few extra breaths to settle her nerves, she worked herself halfway to hyperventilation. A totally useless state. She needed to develop a rational plan and then act on it.

First, she would read the card and confirm her worst fears. Then she'd call the cops and alert them to her situation. Last, she would work her tail off to update the security on her house and her car.

Standing in her foyer and quaking in her high heels served zero purpose.

She wrenched open the front door and hauled the flowers inside. No way would she read the card outdoors where she could have a coronary out in the open. She'd do her hyperventilating in the privacy of her own home, thank you very much.

After edging the heavy arrangement into the hall, she dropped it on the floor and felt around for the card. Snagging the crisp white envelope, she backed toward the bench where Summer's fabric samples still lay. She clutched the burgundy velvet to her like a security blanket, as if she could wring some metaphysical connection with her new friend simply by holding on to the fabric.

And knowing Summer, she would probably say such a thing was possible.

Had Jimmy found her? Was he angry that she'd left New York and robbed him of his daily stalker routine? She yanked the card out of the envelope and read:

Thanks for covering for me. You're the best. Mel.

Melvin?

Her brain scurried to adjust her thinking. She was still safe. Jimmy wouldn't be skulking around Ocean Drive looking for her. Or at least, not yet.

Her relief that her ex-boyfriend wasn't on her trail was quickly overcome by anger that her crooked former stepfather would send her such a sentiment. He thought she was covering for him?

On what planet exactly did he see that happening?

Steam hissed through her, a welcome change after the fear that had gripped her moments before.

The rat bastard.

How dare he assume she'd aid and abet a criminal—even if she *had* called him daddy for a few years when she was still young and naïve? And what could he possibly have construed as covering for him when she'd been very forthcoming with Aidan from the start?

Hell's bells. She was going to have to show the note to Aidan.

And she couldn't put it off until tomorrow, not when

it could be important to his investigation. For all she knew, maybe he could track down how the flowers had been sent and find out something about Mel's location that way.

According to Aidan, they didn't give out those FBI badges to every Joe Blow on the street corner after all.

He'd said he was going to make a stop at the club today. He ought to be easy enough to find.

So even though she'd only just parted company with the man, she had no choice but to track him down again so she could spend more time with him on her only day off this week.

She'd never been a betting woman given her run-ins with Mel's swindler buddies as a youth. But she'd love to know what the odds were that she'd be able to walk away from the man twice in one day without touching him.

Gathering up her purse, she shoved the florist's card in a side compartment. Luckily, she also needed to make a quick stop at police headquarters and beef up her home security. Just in case.

There wouldn't be any time to contemplate Aidan's killer bod.

Or his sexy voice.

Or his willingness to play lovers' games with her.

She had serious business to take care of today and no run-in with Aidan would make her forget it. Once she revealed her news about Mel contacting her, she'd discuss her recurring problems with her ex at the police station.

And then, by God, she'd be ready to claim her future—free and clear of dangerous men.

SOMETHING ABOUT BRIANNE'S flowers didn't sit well with Aidan. Too bad he didn't realize what it was until he looked past the dumb-ass jealousy that had been gnawing at him ever since he pulled out of her driveway.

He was already prowling the dimly lit back halls of Club Paradise when he finally realized what bothered him.

The hang-up phone call she'd received earlier that day.

Hadn't he told himself—and her—he was going to be on the lookout for her in light of that phone call? Yet it hadn't occurred to him that those flowers she received might be connected to the phone call. And the only reason he hadn't put the two things together in his mind was because he was too busy envying the guy who'd caught Bri's eye.

Could he be a bigger idiot?

Suddenly, he couldn't cross his fingers enough that those damn orchids had been from an admirer. Far better that than if they were from some creep who was bothering her.

He yanked a phone from the pocket of his suit jacket and jabbed in the numbers for her cell. Damned if at that same moment, a phone didn't start ringing from somewhere behind him in the semidarkness.

Standing utterly still he waited. Listened.

A feminine voice purred through the receiver and through the echoing corridor under construction.

"Hello?"

That throaty voice would send shivers down a man's spine if the subject at hand hadn't been so important.

"Where are you?"

She gasped. A quick intake of breath that enabled him to locate her. Two doors down behind some scaffolding.

"We need to talk." He spoke into the receiver and then folded the phone closed as he spotted her.

Her pale skin stood out in the shadows, her arms bared by the brown silk tank top she wore from earlier in the day. Although daylight still shone outside, the interior corridors of the hotel lacked windows. The lights seemed to be on some energy-saving mode where they only came on when the lounge was open downstairs or when construction work was underway.

She spotted him too, jabbing the off button on her phone and stuffing it into the slim briefcase she carried. She looked a little frazzled, which in light of her usual perfect appearance meant she had a few windblown hairs breezing around her neck. And she had her shoes off.

"Are you okay?" He studied her, refusing to let his emotions do his thinking for him this time around. The only unusual thing he could find was that she was carrying her high heels instead of wearing them on her feet. With most women, that wouldn't surprise him at the end of the day, but it seemed a bit informal for the woman raised by Palm Beach's answer to Emily Post. "What gives with the shoes?"

"I was trying to be quiet because I knew you wouldn't be expecting anyone else to be here. And no, everything's not okay." She thrust her hand forward to give him a piece of paper. "Read this."

Apparently she'd been sneaking up on him, thanks

to her damn camera system. He might have grumbled about that a little if he hadn't been so concerned about what had upset her.

The paper was actually a tiny envelope. Like a florist's card.

Tearing out the note inside he read a couple of short lines that did an excellent job of incriminating Brianne.

Thanks for covering for me. You're the best. Mel.

"I don't know what he's referring to." She met his gaze head-on. Her voice never wavered. "But I wanted to give you this in case you could trace the flower order and find out where it came from."

The envelope lacked a business name, but that many orchids had to be a memorable order for any store. Assuming they were obtained locally. "I'll look into it."

He shoved the card in his pocket. The evidence would keep. Right now, he needed to interrogate a woman full of mysteries who could probably help him a hell of a lot more. He slung one arm around the metal pole of the scaffolding, anchoring himself in case she got fired up about this.

"I know you're not going to want to answer this question, Brianne, but it's related to the investigation and doesn't have a damn thing to do with us personally. I need to know who you thought the flowers were from in the first place. Did you suspect they were from Mel and that's why you wanted me out of there so fast?"

Her forehead wrinkled as if she exercised great effort to follow his logic. "Why would I spend my day off hunting you down to show this to you if I thought they were from him in the first place? I could have saved myself a lot of time if I'd just handed you the card while you were on my front doorstep.''

''Maybe you had an attack of conscience?'' Hell, he didn't know. She probably still harbored some affection for the guy. From what Aidan had gathered, Mel had provided her with the most stable father figure she'd had in her life. ''It's not like I'd think you belonged on the Most Wanted list if you tried to give him a hand.''

''Could we not talk about this here?'' She glanced around the hallway and then down at her mini viewing screen on the pseudo-watch she wore whenever she was at the club. ''We do have cleaning staff and construction people who work when we're closed.''

Spying a door not two feet from her elbow, he steered her toward it. ''Do you have a master key or do you want to see my lock picking skills in action?''

She sighed, pressed a button on her little computer pad and the green light flared beside the doorknob.

Aidan shoved his way into a room filled with lavender silk curtains around the bed and more pastel silk hangings all over the walls. Covered rattan baskets served as low tables while fat silky cushions dotted the floor. The only light fixtures were wall sconces in the shape of candelabra.

''It's a harem.'' And he had to think he wasn't the only guy who would find it a bit of a challenge to crack cases in a harem.

''Summer's calling it the Pasharina's Palace so far, but we're trying to convince her there are only pashas and not pasharinas. If any great names for the room come to you, by all means let me know and I'll throw them into the pot.'' She stood amid the flowing silks and seemed quite content to discuss a new topic, but Aidan needed a few more answers first.

''I'll get back to you. Now, can you tell me who you thought the flowers were from since you didn't think they were from Melvin?'' He searched for a place to sit, but all the lush pillows and sensual fabrics begged more intimacy than either he or Brianne could afford.

Her jaw flexed. Tightened. Pursing her lips, she glared at him for two slow heartbeats before she said a word. ''I thought they were from a guy in New York. An old boyfriend.''

That would do for a start anyway. ''Can I have his name?''

''I need a damn alibi to receive flowers?''

''Damn it, Brianne, don't make this any harder than it already is. Just give me a name and we'll leave it at that.''

''I don't want to leave it at that. I want you to find Melvin and lock him up so I can get on with my life. What I'm objecting to is having my past unearthed for the sake of a flower alibi.'' She sounded rattled and he hated knowing he'd disrupted her life that much.

Correction, he hated Melvin for dumping his crimes in her lap while he lived the high life in Guadalajara or the Cayman Islands or any one of ten thousand other remote havens.

''His name is James Vanderwalk and he lives on the lower West Side. Our breakup ranked as a monumental disaster in his life and I'm eager to put some distance between us.'' She seemed to settle down with the admission. Tossing aside her shoes and her briefcase, she strode across the light-colored carpet to a wet bar surrounded by small potted trees and hanging plants. A desert oasis.

''And does this James guy know you're living down here now?'' He definitely needed to know more about a relationship that still had the power to rattle Brianne. The woman was hell on wheels *and* a security genius.

It seemed as though any guy who could upset her that much had to be more than just your run-of-the-mill jerk.

She tugged a bottle of wine from a hidden shelf of the wet bar, or maybe she'd gotten it from one of those in-room vending machines. Either way, she set it on the bar and started unwinding the paper seal from around the neck.

''I hope like hell he doesn't know I'm down here, Aidan, and trust me, it's the kind of story that requires a drink with the telling.''

He didn't like the sound of that one damn bit. In fact, the hair on the back of his neck stood straight up while his fists urged his brain to find out how fast they could lay waste to this James guy.

But he wasn't a street thug unless the situation called for it. He'd grown up in neighborhoods a hell of a lot tougher than anything South Beach had to offer and he'd managed to haul himself up out of those years by keeping his nose clean whenever possible. Still, the thought of Brianne having to defend herself against an obsessive lunatic made his fists clench.

Somehow, he shoved those thoughts aside enough

to cross the room and join her at the bar. Right now, he was going to find out a hell of a lot more than how fast he could tank one James Vanderwalk.

Seeing a definite exception to his no drinking on the job rule, he yanked two glasses from a cabinet behind the bar and stood them on the counter.

"You're not leaving until you tell me everything."

10

How often did a woman hear an invitation like that?

Brianne knew Aidan was trying to pull the intimidating FBI-guy routine on her with his "you're not leaving until you tell me everything" spiel. But she couldn't remember any man in her entire life—and that included numerous boyfriends and several stand-in fathers—being so adamant about hearing what she had to say.

Pouring the wine into their glasses as they stood in the lushly appointed harem room, she reminded herself that part of the reason Aidan wanted to hear about her past was because of his case. But as she handed him his merlot and their eyes met in the flickering light of the electric candelabra scattered about the room, Brianne saw more than professional interest in his gaze.

He wanted to know more about her.

What could it hurt to unburden herself just a little? Aidan's shoulders looked as though they could stand the weight.

"It's not a pretty story," she warned him, visually searching the room for a place to sit that wasn't draped in silk and satin. Had it ever occurred to Summer to install bar stools in a room with a bar? "And I guess

I'm going to have to concede today as a loss for getting anything done. Do you have a few minutes?''

''Sure. Let's grab a seat and—'' Their eyes fell on the bed at the same moment. Draped in hangings of light purple silk and situated next to a miniature stone fountain, the high mattress surrounded by pillows ranked as the most substantial piece of furniture in the room. ''I take it pasharinas aren't fond of chairs?''

''So it would seem. What if we just sit on the floor and we can use the—'' She stared at the bed and the pristine white spread. And quickly conjured a vision of her and Aidan rolling, writhing on that cool, clean expanse of silky fabric. ''—*that* as a backrest.''

Had she really just suggested they step within five feet of a mattress?

Aidan nodded slowly—as if under protest.

But she'd never been the kind of woman to back down. And damn it, if she had to tell this painful story, she would be at least *physically* comfortable in the process.

Plunking down on the carpet, Brianne tugged two rattan baskets over from the foot of the bed and dropped them in between her and the spot Aidan had chosen a few feet away.

Tan and smooth, the covered baskets measured about the size of hatboxes and would make the perfect coffee table for the wine. They also created a nifty physical barrier to Aidan just in case she felt herself weakening in his enticing male presence.

She'd learned a long time ago that a girl didn't necessarily need to be born with great willpower and emotional reserves to have strength. A strong woman knew how to stack the deck in her favor.

Or, in this case, the baskets.

Aidan peered at her across the rattan divide and gulped back half his wine. "This guy never hurt you, Brianne." He stated it as fact, as if by sheer force of his will, he could make it so. Then, when she didn't respond right away, he raised an eyebrow. "Did he?"

"Not in a physical way. But he definitely dragged me through the wringer emotionally." What a mess that had been. "He's a musician. And I guess that accounts for part of the reason I found myself drawn to him. He seemed like a more emotionally intuitive person. Sort of the antithesis of me."

"Not true."

Brianne rolled her eyes. Sipped her wine. Welcomed the warmth of the drink in her throat before she reached the next phase of her story. "Either way, I soon discovered that what I'd perceived as sensitivity was actually just one phase of extreme mood swings. When I told him things weren't working out between us, he turned even creepier."

Aidan stiffened. No amount of rattan would disguise the light shift and ripple of muscles beneath his suit jacket. His jaw flexed. "Creepy in what way?"

"He started calling my apartment, my office, my cell all day, every day. I changed my own phones, but I couldn't do anything about my work number. He'd wait for me outside my building, follow me home. He wrote me lots of weird letters, song lyrics—" she hesitated, wishing she didn't have to admit much more of the nightmare "—and poetic threats. Beautifully scripted, lovingly worded pleas for compliance so he didn't have to hurt me.''

"Jesus, Brianne. Why didn't you show any of this to the cops?''

She bristled. And welcomed an opportunity to bristle, actually, because thinking about that whole scary chapter of her life tended to make her ill. "I did show all of it to the cops.''

"There's no record of any of it.'' Perhaps he noticed her glare because he hastened to add, "not that you were ever on my suspect list, Bri, but I definitely did a search for information on you in case Melvin sought you out. And I can tell you for damn sure there's no record of you lodging any complaints with the police in New York.''

Well, wasn't that just perfect? "So if I'd been found strangled on my doorstep, they wouldn't have had a clue as to whom to arrest, I suppose? That's incredibly reassuring.'' Vaguely, she wondered what else Aidan had unearthed about her in his search. She tilted her head back against the white satin bedspread and allowed the cool material to tickle her neck and shoulders. "I have to say, they didn't seem all that impressed with threats written in rhyming stanzas.''

"They're going to be pretty freaking sorry they weren't more impressed when I call them tonight and raise hell over there.'' He turned sideways to face her, sweeping aside the gossamer bed veils and anchoring himself with one long arm across the mattress. "And I can assure you we'll know exactly where this Vanderwalk guy is by tomorrow.''

Warmth swirled through her, a tingly, unfamiliar

feeling of having someone else look out for her. "Thank you. I've been meaning to get in touch with the police down here to at least alert them to the situation. I don't think Jimmy would ever leave New York to seek me out, but then again…"

"Never underestimate your enemy. Can you define the nature of the threats he made against you?"

"They were pretty vague for the most part. He never spelled out any particular form of violence, just expressed a desire *not* to hurt me. Of course, as soon as he'd say that, he'd invariably follow it up with some sort of line about how I provided him with no alternatives." And she'd hated the fear that instilled in her.

Her whole life she'd prided herself on confronting challenges, charging through her male-dominated industry armed with cool professionalism and the drive to get a job done. But those months where Jimmy had been following her around, sending her the letters, she'd retreated from everything.

When the opportunity arose in South Beach for her to pitch in at Club Paradise, she'd jumped at the chance to escape the prison her life had become. And even though she was pretty certain she'd have moved to Florida no matter what, it bothered her that the decision had been made for her because she'd been living in fear.

"So there were never any more specific threats made?" Jaw clenched, eyes intense, Aidan had morphed into investigative mode—asking questions and looking for clues. For once, his job didn't seem dangerous so much as noble.

"Well, come to think of it, one of the creepiest letters he sent said something about my defection being like a knife in his heart and how he hoped I'd never experience that kind of pain.'' In a fit of paranoia, she'd dumped every kitchen knife she owned into the drawer under her oven. Surely no psychotic stalker would think to look for a knife there should he attempt to attack her in her home?

The string of curses Aidan ripped loose could have made a sailor blush. Undaunted by the phenomenon, Brianne only wished the New York police had been half so enraged on her account.

When he finished his wine and seemed to have himself under control again, he looked only semi-apoplectic.

''Do you have these letters?'' Maybe Aidan had gleaned that the memory still unsettled her because he retrieved the bottle of wine from the bar and then sat back down to refill her glass. His movements were stiff, his gestures tautly controlled.

''I left a few of the early originals with the cops in New York, but I still have the note about the knife in my chest.'' She'd stashed that one at the back of her closet.

''If you give it to me, I'll make sure it's recorded in police files.'' His fingers toyed restlessly with the edge of a scarf tossed across the foot of the bed. Brianne happened to know the gauzy white scarf was part of a belly dancing costume Summer wanted to hang on one of the walls, but all she'd managed to acquire so far were the headpiece and veil.

Watching Aidan's big hands adjust the line of beads across the bottom of the veil did shivery things to her insides even though she knew he flipped the fabric back and forth out of thinly controlled frustration.

"Why didn't you tell me about all this before?" His gray gaze pierced hers in the soft glow of the electric candlelight, his jaw flexing rapidly. "For that matter, why the hell didn't you pick up a phone in New York and utilize your FBI contact to leverage some help for yourself, Bri? I would have—" He shook his head, huffed out an aggravated sigh. "You should have called me."

"Not in a million years would it have occurred to me to call the guy who investigated my former stepfather's crimes to ask for help." She'd worked hard to put Aidan Maddock—and her boundary-pushing behavior with him—out of her mind once she started college. "As for why I didn't say anything about it the last couple of days... I guess I've been preoccupied with getting the club off the ground." Normally, she would have stopped there, but the wine on an empty stomach seemed to rob her of her usual reserve. Her smooth control. "And maybe I was a little embarrassed to admit I'd gotten involved with a guy like that. It scares me to think I'm turning into Pauline."

"Embarrassed? I can't believe you just said that. You'd ream out any of your girlfriends if they ever said they were too embarrassed to point the finger at a loser-ass stalker. And pardon the clueless guy over here, Bri, but what does being embarrassed have to do with your mother?"

"She's got a bad habit of choosing guys who are no good for her. That's always driven me crazy about her and now I'm convinced I'm following that same self-destructive path in her size five footsteps.'' She finished her second glass and peered down at the miniature monitor screen on her wrist—the remote monitoring system was rotating views of various rooms depending on the time. Now, she was able to access the darkened dance club, the Ocean Drive entrance to the club, an elevator bank and…the Pasharina's Palace.

Complete with a lovely view of her and Aidan lounging next to one another on the floor.

She wanted to turn off the lighted display, but something about the intimate picture captured her director's eye. The lighting in the room flickered with suggestive intimacy. The couple on the floor floated on a backdrop of washed-out colors—barely-there lavender bed hangings, the white bedspread in the background, a pale carpet below them.

''Everything okay?'' Aidan's long arm was already breaching the rattan basket barrier to brush her wrist and catch a glimpse. Brianne shut off the display.

She didn't have to wonder if he'd seen the image on the screen. The new heat in his glance told her he had.

''You're going to get in a hell of a lot of legal trouble if you rent out hotel rooms with video cameras in them, Brianne.'' His voice hit a gravelly note that rumbled right through her.

''The cameras in private rooms will be removed before we open. I just move them around among the rooms Summer will be working on so I can make sure she's safe. And so she can act out her lunch order for me when she gets hungry.'' Of course, her charades were always a challenge given she ate things like tofu on rye and bean sprout salad. "The cameras will be available on a closed circuit for making private videos once we reopen, however."

He lifted a brow. "Which brings me back to an interesting point we started to discuss earlier today before we went to your mother's. How exactly are you marketing Club Paradise given all the erotic statues and provocative themes? I thought I heard you were leaving behind the couples theme with the new renovations." Loosening his tie, he sent her a look that would have flash-fried a lesser woman.

As it stood, she was merely a little singed around the edges.

"Actually, we are stressing the singles angle with the revamped club. None of the new owners were too excited about the schmaltzy lovebirds logo on every blanket, towel and bathrobe in the place." Her throat went dry as the atmosphere in the room shifted, thickened.

"So instead of catering to people who are in love, you're creating the ultimate setting for people looking to hook up. No wonder you're calling it Club Paradise. People are going to flock here in droves."

Brianne watched as Aidan flicked open the top button of his shirt. He'd ditched his jacket earlier, maybe when he went to retrieve the bottle of wine.

The man looked damn good in a tie.

Crisp cotton outlined his sinewy arms, stretched across his chest. She knew if she tunneled her fingers through his shirt she'd find solid, defined abs and more tan skin. Not that she could reach him even if she had allowed herself to touch him.

Some genius with no clue about sex drive had put a wall of baskets between them.

"My years as a director assured me sex sells." Sex also made even the smartest of women do stupid things. Like scale perfectly good barriers to get to the object of their lust. And Aidan sure looked tempting right about now. "Or at least the promise of sex sells."

"Frankly, you have me sold." He ran a finger under a collar now considerably loosened. "Brianne, I think I'd better go check in with the police station, or make some calls before things get…complicated."

No.

She'd been so damn sure they shouldn't be together again, but after sharing her past with Aidan she felt just a little vulnerable. Emotions she'd tamped down for too long churned at the surface, leaving her confused, restless. She wanted Aidan—needed him—to relieve that edginess. If she were completely honest with herself, she had to admit, she also needed to borrow his strength, indulge in his warmth on a night of confessions that had left her defenseless.

She ran an idle fingertip over the ridge of woven rattan that formed her makeshift table. Had she really thought that being strong had to do with knowing when to erect barriers?

Maybe sometimes being a strong woman meant knowing when to tear them down.

"I think we passed the complicated stage in this relationship ten years ago. And just in case you're at all concerned about what I want right now, I don't care about how fast you contact the police or how soon we learn where my psycho ex is hanging out." She took a deep breath and shoved aside the basket closest to her. "Between visiting my mother, hearing from Mel and then sharing my darkest secret with you, I'm feeling a little unsteady. And I just keep thinking maybe I'd be able to settle down and pull it together if only I could indulge the one thing I've been thinking about since we walked in this room."

Aidan probably never suspected. Freud had searched half his life for the answer to what women want. How could she expect a bachelor FBI agent with a dating track record as spotty as Melvin Baxter's income tax returns would ever be able to answer that?

He quirked a lazy brow in her direction. "Which is?"

"I think we ought to christen the Pasharina's Palace with sweaty, no-holds-barred sex."

SHE'D BEEN THINKING *that?*

Hell and damn.

Fascinated, Aidan watched in a state of frozen lust as Brianne gave the baskets separating them a final nudge with her knee. She rose up on all fours to close the distance between them.

Strictly speaking, he supposed she was crawling her way across the carpet. But "crawling" hardly did her slow prowl justice. She covered the terrain on all fours with enough steamy attitude to fog his contact lenses.

He needed to check out her stalker. Protect her, not sleep with her. Damn it, he'd been prepared to be noble and do the upstanding thing.

But then again, it wouldn't be noble to duck out on a woman who'd just admitted to feeling vulnerable.

His need to protect her slowly shifted into the dawning realization that maybe if he claimed her tonight he'd be able to look out for her all the more. Possibly that thought sprang to mind because she hovered mere inches away, her unconventional position giving him an incredible view down her blouse.

"I'm driving you home later." If he had to cave tonight, he would at least make that clear up front. "No changing your mind just because you decide to give me the boot in the middle of the night."

She ducked her head to brush her lips along his neck, under his jaw. "Maybe if you please me, I won't be inclined to boot you out."

"I hope you aren't going to suggest for a moment that I didn't please you last time." The silk of her tank top slid over his dress shirt, her breasts a soft weight beneath the fabric. "But if that's a challenge, lady, you can bet your gadget collection I'm taking you up on it." Only Brianne would issue sexual challenges while experiencing vulnerability.

Then again, maybe her sudden sexy attitude was simply a cover for deeper insecurities. Hurts.

Ah damn, he didn't want to think that.

Couldn't stand the idea of someone hurting her below the surface where he hadn't been able to see it right away.

She licked a path down his throat to the V of his shirt but Aidan gently gripped her upper arms and righted her so she faced him on her knees.

"Are you sure about this, Bri?" He'd probably overstepped his bounds a bit with the strip search. He sure as hell wasn't going to play games with her while she still reeled from all the baggage—the fear—someone else had dumped on her.

Her green eyes shifted from dull jade to bright emerald. ''I don't want to be alone tonight.'' She blinked quickly. Maintained his gaze. ''I know I'm engaging in emotional decision-making here, but I want to feel good again. Sexy. Whole.''

Her simple request slid under his radar, past his libido and wound around him with gentle insistence. He didn't know that he was equal to the task. ''Sexy'' he could handle backward and forward. ''Whole'' was another matter entirely. But if she entrusted him with herself tonight—and he knew with certainty she was only talking about tonight—he would make damn sure to give it his best shot.

And no way in hell would he screw up that small display of her trust by ducking out to call the South Beach PD. Somehow, that faith meant far more to him than he'd ever suspected it could.

The hunger he'd been fighting today ever since he'd found her clutching burgundy velvet between her fingers and gazing at pictures of erotic statuary now came roaring back to life. He drew her down to him and pressed his mouth to hers. He kissed her too hard, held her too tightly.

Still, her lips softened beneath his. He groaned helplessly as need swept over him, hot and fierce. This wasn't supposed to happen tonight. After she'd written off their last time together as a minor setback, he'd been determined to maintain professional boundaries with Brianne.

But all bets were off. She'd come to him, had confided in him. Wanted him.

Her body molded to his. The ramrod-straight spine that normally marked her movements now arched above him. She'd dissolved against him where he still sprawled on the floor, one thigh brushing his.

She *wanted* him.

Did it make him ten times an idiot to be so floored about that when she'd fully admitted her decision-making process might be flawed because of runaway emotions?

His fingers smoothed over the small of her back, the sweet slope of her bottom through silky pants. "I want you." He mouthed the words against her lips, unwilling to lose the taste of her for even a second.

Her hand skimmed the taut muscle of his abs to graze the hard, aching length of him through his fly. Her lips were swollen against his, but she paused enough to whisper back, "I know."

Those fingers flexed around him. Sent him scavenging for breath and stole the last reserves of his restraint.

He flipped their positions, never breaking their kiss. She met the thrust of his tongue, sighed with pleasure. His hands slipped and slid all over the silky material of her blouse and pants. Impatient to touch skin, he reached for the waistband of her slacks and withdrew the hem of her shirt. Tunneling beneath the fabric, he splayed his palm over her belly, smoothed his hand up to the insubstantial lace cups of her bra. He peeled down the straps and exposed her breasts.

"I want to taste you." He shoved up her blouse, tugged it off her shoulders. "Need to taste you."

Nudging aside the remnants of her black lace bra, he lowered his head to her breast and drew her into his mouth. Deeply.

She let out a soft cry as he drew on her, her fingers tangling in his hair, her body arched and willing beneath him. Some last gasp of his conscience told him that she wanted to feel sexy when all he could think about was complete, immediate possession. Claiming her totally for himself so no man could ever threaten her again.

Yet she writhed and wriggled below him, her skin as fiery with the heat of pure need as his.

He unhooked the front clasp of her bra and let the lace fabric fall away from her. Kissing a trail between her breasts, his mouth found her other peaked nipple and suckled her. Savored her.

Never had he wanted a woman this much. Ever. The scent of her filled his nostrils and made him edgy for more.

And he planned to take much more.

He only had one thing to clarify first.

Staring down at Brianne he found a woman in the throes of passion. Head tipped back, hair tangled and tousled, body flushed with desire. In that provocative condition she probably hadn't given much thought to their security in this room with a video camera rolling.

"Are you sure no one else has access to your office or your videotapes, Brianne?" He watched her passion-clouded eyes blink through confusion, but damn it, this was important. "If you think there's any chance someone else might see us, I'll find a way to disarm the camera. Because I can guarantee you someone's going to get an eye full in about ten more seconds."

11

THE VIDEO CAMERA.

Brianne's eyes went to the device in the corner of the room. How could she have forgotten that her every greedy response to Aidan's kisses was being recorded?

"You can't disarm it. Just throw a shirt over it or something." The damn thing had already seen too much. The slim black electronic gadget had been privy to Brianne's weakest moments, her request that Aidan stay with her.

But more than that, the camera would have caught the expression on her face when he touched her, the passionate rapture she'd experienced at his kiss. She had the feeling she'd be haunted for a long time by the footage that had already been taped.

Her eyes followed Aidan across the room, his tall, muscular body a very pleasing sight as he scooped up his jacket and tossed it over the lens. Her mouth watered as he stretched up to make sure the jacket would stay in position. Between the squared, broad shoulders, the tapered back leading to narrow hips and the butt of taut muscle that led a woman to think about the power—no, endurance—he could put behind his sexual maneuvers... Brianne wondered how she'd kept her hands off him all day.

And that was just the rear view.

She considered tackling him in the middle of the floor when he turned around and she snagged a glimpse at the front of him.

So fine.

And all mine.

As soon as the words formed in her brain she wondered where they had come from. Surely she'd only meant ''all mine'' in a physical, temporary sense. Didn't she?

But then he was over her, scooping her up in his arms like her five-foot-eleven body weighed no more than a sack of potatoes. Allowing her eyes to fall shut, she clung to his neck and held on tight until he edged her through the silky purple bed hangings and lowered her in the middle of the white satin bed.

He wasted no time easing down the zipper of her slacks or peeling them away from her skin. When she lay there in front of him, naked but for her black lace panties, he slipped one hand beneath the low-cut waistband and gathered the fabric in a knot in his hand.

She shivered in anticipation as he held that scrap of material, knowing exactly what he had in mind. She'd probably fantasized about it aloud one of the many times she'd tried to seduce him as a teenage hellion. Now with one yank the scrap of lace tore free, leaving her totally exposed.

Her hair fanned out on the spread, the cool fabric tickling her bare, hot shoulders. And at that moment, she realized Aidan had already succeeded in making her feel sexy tonight. She reached for him to tell him as much, but her fingers found only empty air. Prying her eyes open, she spied him just outside the sheer curtains surrounding the bed, removing his clothes.

Mmm.

The only thing she enjoyed more than the front and rear view of Aidan Maddock was catching sight of the front and rear view while gorgeously, deliciously naked.

Rolling on her side, she stretched to touch his bare thigh through the sheer silk as he ditched the last of his garments. The heat of that hard muscle jumped across the fabric to singe her hand while the light hair on his leg bristled through to rasp against her palm.

The guttural growl he made encouraged her. Called her curious hand to touch that jutting male arousal with her silk-covered fingers. If his thigh had been hot, his erection was molten. And swollen. And incredibly thick.

Closing her fingers around him, she stroked the length of him, up and down. Watched in rapt fascination as he hissed a long breath between his teeth.

She wanted him. Wanted *this* with an intensity that frightened her.

Aidan locked her wrist in his grip, restrained her from touching him any more. She didn't need to ask why. The fierce look in his eyes, the determined set of his jaw told her he was a man on a mission of conquest and that her body would be the next terrain on his list.

By the time he wrenched the curtains apart and climbed over her on the bed, her thighs were already parting. Ready.

In her mind, she whispered thanks to him for rolling on a condom at that moment. She couldn't be entirely certain that those words ever made it to her lips. And then she had no hope of talking as he dipped a finger inside her, tested the slick heat of her.

That intimate touch provided welcome sensual relief from the hunger that filled her, even as it made her crave all the more. Her hips arched toward him as her body convulsed around him with a little spasm, a luscious precursor of the sweet release that awaited her.

Skimming her hands up his strong arms, she absorbed the caged tension of restless muscles and hot skin. She glanced at his face and found his steely gray gaze directed on her. He hadn't missed a moment of her lush, heady response to him. And something about the intense nature of his eyes communicated he understood exactly where she wanted to go tonight—sensually speaking—and that he knew just how to get her there.

She arched up to kiss him, to taste him, but he was already leaning down to her.

He nudged aside her hair with his hand, whispered in her ear. "Is tonight a really bad night for sexual adventure?"

The question hovered there, hot and suggestive and full of possibilities.

"Is it ever a bad night for sexual adventure?" she whispered back, lifting her hips to graze his body with her own.

"I'm serious, Bri." His voice rasped against her ear, an edgy growl that meant business. "I think all the harem stuff is starting to go to my head."

She lowered her hand to touch him, ran two teasing

fingers up the hard length of his cock. "You want me to belly dance for you?"

So maybe she knew she was pushing her luck with a man on the edge. Maybe she wanted to push her luck.

Aidan didn't disappoint.

By some feat of male strength, he had her flipped facedown on the mattress inside of two seconds. And in spite of the he-man tactics of tossing her around, he'd been kind enough to jab a pillow underneath her.

Leaving him hard, hot and obviously horny as hell behind her.

Mmm.

His mouth waited inches from her ear, his body sprawled out on top of her while his arms sustained most of his weight. "No belly dancing required. I'm only asking that you indulge the onslaught of male domination fantasies the harem tent is inspiring."

Desire scorched through her even as Aidan's arms banded around her. He lifted her hips, positioned himself between her thighs and then eased inside her, inch by glorious inch.

Brianne anchored herself on the bed with extended arms, arching back to meet him as he took her from behind in the most dominant male position. He held her to him, guided her body down to meet his with every slow thrust.

His other hand took more liberties. First tweaking her hard, aching nipples, then moving lower to touch between her legs. To rub slow, sweet circles with his finger while his thrusts gained speed.

Her climax hit her like a lightning bolt, a fierce, almost frightening shock of spasms that rocked her to her core. She cried out his name, almost wept with the joy of that sharp pleasure.

But he wasn't finished.

No, the male domination fantasy had apparently been more for her benefit than his. And when she was ever able to breathe or speak again she would let him know how much her body had appreciated it.

Right now, she was being gently turned around as Aidan rolled underneath her. Putting them face to face again.

And this time, she was on top and in charge.

Still limp from the orgasm that had spun her world on its ear, Brianne didn't have a clue what she'd do with her newfound position of power, but she knew one thing.

Aidan wouldn't be sorry he'd given her control.

TRADITIONALLY, AIDAN HAD NEVER been the kind of guy to take the mattress. He asserted himself in every arena of his life and the bedroom was no different.

But between the strip search in her office the other night and the wild interlude they'd just shared on the bed, Aidan knew he needed to let Brianne run the show. Exercise a little sensual power of her own.

He just hoped he'd last long enough to let her. He'd been hanging by a thread ever since her body had tensed with the first tremors of her release and if she moved so much as an eyelash right now—or in the next ten seconds—he'd be toast.

Luckily, she remained sprawled across his chest, her breath still hitching on the occasional shudder.

Damn, but that pleased him.

When she levered herself up on outstretched arms to face him, her swollen lips, her long tousled hair, her flushed skin gave her the look of a wanton angel. The upside to taking the mattress position for a guy had to be the view. Brianne looked so good it hurt.

Fighting the urge to flip her on her back and lick every square inch of that gorgeous body of hers, Aidan watched as she lifted herself off him just enough to tease him. Then her eyes fluttered closed as she eased back down the hard length of him so slowly he thought he'd explode from anticipation.

He let her set the pace even though it was killing him, giving himself over to her more subtle approach. She bent to kiss his chest, her tongue flicking out along his shoulder and down to his pecs while she rode him with slow, painstaking thoroughness.

Blood pounded through his ears at ten times the speed of Brianne's seductive movements. She licked and nipped him, and once when he made the mistake of gripping her hips to urge her onward, she gave his shoulder a playful warning bite.

But she needed this, damn it. This night, this control. And Aidan wanted to be the only man to give it to her.

When he felt himself losing grip on his restraint, he reached between them to touch her, to propel her once again toward her own provocative pinnacle. But she pinned him to the bed with her delicate hands, using her will and not her strength to communicate her wants.

And she had every intention of driving him over the edge on his own while she stared down at him with fascinated green eyes.

Definitely not a he-man way to go down for the count. But with each roll of her hips he had less and less choice until he lost his mind, his control, and a little slice out of his heart to a woman who didn't need his brand of trouble in her life right now.

HOURS LATER, HE WATCHED Brianne twist a stray piece of white veil around her finger. Actually, she'd told him at one point the fabric belonged to a dancing costume that would be available along with the harem room. Right before she'd donned the veil and demonstrated a few moves for him.

Their night had been amazing to the point of being downright scary. They shouldn't have a damn thing in common, yet they'd found things to talk and laugh about when they weren't actively setting the sheets on fire.

Sooner or later, he'd have to arrest her former stepfather and no matter what she said to the contrary, Aidan had the feeling she would be affected by that more than even she realized. That would be a blow to any relationship they might have been able to work out.

Add to that the fact that Aidan needed to check in with his informant at the club, the too-eager cigarette girl, Daisy. He had the feeling he didn't stand a snowball's chance in hell of avoiding Brianne's all-seeing security camera for that meeting and he'd have to contend with the fallout from that. His ex-wife had never understood the need to talk to people, spend so much time on the street and on the job for his investigations either. But he couldn't have changed his commitment to his work if he tried. The need to bring justice had been implanted in him way back in the days of watching superheroes on Saturday morning cartoons.

Of course, if his meeting with Daisy didn't push Brianne away from him for good, then there was the fact that he planned to involve himself knee-deep in the matter of this stalker ex-boyfriend of hers. No doubt that was going to ruffle a few of her feathers too.

But even as he saw the inevitable crash and burn of their relationship, Aidan couldn't resist pulling her closer now. Her body felt so right, fit so perfectly beside his. Her hair set fire to everything it came in contact with, the red strands like bright flames licking over his arm, his chest, the bed.

Brianne came to him, settling her head on his chest as she continued to wrap and unwrap the sheer white veil from around her hand. "You don't think Mel is still in Florida and delivered those flowers himself, do you? When we went to set up the legal terms of Club Paradise and dissolved the former ownership, the lawyers agreed Melvin and his Rat Pack crew were all out of the country by now."

"If they had any sense they'd be out of the country. But I'm banking on Mel's greed being as strong as ever. I think he'll return soon if he's not in town already. He's going to want the money in your mother's account."

"I could put in a few phone calls to flower shops in the morning and see if they have any record of the orchids being ordered."

"You'd be willing to do that to help me out?" Aidan shifted on to his side so that he could look her in the eye. "I had you pegged for the kind of woman who would never voluntarily walk within spitting range of the FBI." Like his ex-wife.

She paused in her fabric twisting, green eyes meeting his in the light cast by the flickering candelabra. Now that the sun had long set, the room took on an even more sensual quality. The gossamer curtains around the bed had a subtle sheen that couldn't be appreciated until the room was illuminated by candlelight.

"I have a lot at stake in this case, too. And I don't mind investigating something as long as it's from the safe haven of my office behind the anonymity of a telephone receiver or an Internet connection." She rolled to her back, pulling away from him in more ways than one. "I only protest the danger of catching criminals. Not the task itself."

In other words, she still found plenty of reasons to object to his job. "Actually, I'm going to put some support staff on the job of tracking down the florist avenue. But thank you."

When she didn't say anything he reached for her, wishing they could escape reality a little longer. Wishing for a lot of other things that probably couldn't be. "What do you say we wait and think about this later in the morning?"

As she sat up, clutching a pillow to her like a satin shield, Aidan realized she was already engaged in a full retreat. "Maybe we don't want to wait. It occurred to me that we could probably check out the activity in the banking account in my mother's name. We might be overlooking something important.''

We? Aidan guessed he was missing something here, some key element to Brianne's angle on their relationship. But even with all his years of field experience, he didn't have a clue what that might be. This struck him as more than just an effort to put distance between them. ''You sure you want to tackle that right now?''

''Definitely.'' She scrambled for her blouse and shoved the torn remnants of her panties into her purse, her movements clipped and hurried. ''We can use the office computer.''

Grudgingly, Aidan forced himself out of the bed, away from the warmth that was Brianne. He already knew her complex scent would cling to him for hours and force him to recall their wild night together. ''That's okay. If we're going to tackle this thing, it makes more sense for me to hit the field while you see what you can find on the computer. I'll call New York and Miami Beach police before I leave here though and make sure this James guy is still in New York.''

Brianne clenched the white dancing veil so tightly in her palm that one of the tiny bells along the fringe popped off and rolled on to the floor. He was going out to mingle with crooks and talk to bad guys on the streets even after her offer to look for leads together from the safety of her office?

As she reassembled her outfit with slow precision, she wished she could rebuild her emotional defenses with half as much thoroughness. In the course of an evening, she'd managed to bare far more than her body to Aidan. Somehow she'd revealed secret fears and insecurities she had never shared with any other man.

And he'd even met her mother, for crying out loud.

She was in too deep, too fast. Even worse, she couldn't think straight when they were in the same room together, which was probably why she felt the sudden need for space. Not so much to send Aidan away as to think clearly, because after the series of romantic mistakes she'd made in her lifetime, she didn't trust her judgment when it came to men. At all.

Her only option as far as she could see would be to run far and fast from this night before her faulty decisions started exploding in her face.

While she scanned the floor of the harem-themed hotel room for her shoes, Aidan studied her from where he still lounged on the bed, his tanned chest a dark contrast to the white bed linens all around him. "You got dressed in record-breaking time. You're not running away from me, are you?"

Damn. Damn. Damn.

Brianne had always been far more outspoken than her polite mother. Furthermore, she'd held her own in blunt speaking with New York's notoriously tough film industry crowd. But Aidan's straightforward approach to what they'd shared tonight still threw her for a loop.

Crossing her fingers that the best defense was a strong offense, she let him have it with both guns. She tossed her hair, shot him her best smoldering look. "You shattered my personal lifetime orgasm record in the first two hours we were together, Aidan. What woman in her right mind would run from that kind of sexual firepower?"

"A woman who's scared of a relationship. You." He eyed her from the bed, her six-foot-four personal psychiatrist.

Brianne reeled from the comment even though she didn't so much as blink. Playing it cool grew increasingly challenging when it came to Aidan, however.

"I didn't know we were contemplating a relationship." The word stuck to her tongue a bit before she managed to speak it aloud. Her heart pounded with a swirl of confused emotions at the thought. "Judging by your shared kisses with a cigarette girl followed by your involvement with me, I hadn't pegged you for a relationship type of guy."

God, she sounded like a cynic. And her flip attitude wasn't even honest. She knew damn well Aidan would at least bring more to a relationship than she ever could. But if she didn't find a way to insert some distance between them—fast—she'd be losing her heart to a man who didn't understand her and who was wretchedly wrong for her.

"I spent three years of the last ten as a married man, Brianne. You could say I tried out relationships in a big way." He swiveled off the bed and planted his long, muscular legs on the floor as casually as if he hadn't just rocked her foundations.

"You?" Brianne turned up the lights in the room— partly to hunt for her shoe and partly to occupy her suddenly nervous hands. "Married?"

"Is that so hard to believe?"

"You just seem so absorbed in your job. But maybe that's because I've never really seen you at a time when you weren't working." Would things have been any different between them if they'd met outside his investigations?

"I met Natalie after a hit-and-run accident." He dressed as he talked, covering up the tanned skin Brianne had kissed, licked, touched. "It wasn't part of a case, I just sort of stumbled on the scene on the way home one night."

That sounded like Aidan. She nodded, curious to hear more even as a twinge of jealousy stabbed through her for the woman who had caught Aidan's eye. She was willing to bet Natalie didn't have a criminal for a stepfather.

"She's a nurse and she had stopped to check on the victim. I got involved so I could make sure the cops were on the way, secure the area. We hit it off right away and I took the plunge a few months later." He slid his tie around his neck, not bothering to knot it. "Eventually she got freaked about my job and called it quits. Not that I blame her."

That she could certainly understand.

"And your divorce hasn't soured you on relationships?" Brianne didn't think she could handle a divorce of her own. She'd weathered enough of Pauline's to know they were sticky, unhappy business.

More importantly, they had the potential to break hearts.

"Call me an optimist." He flashed her a sexy grin and took a step closer. The heat of his body reminded her of all they'd shared tonight. "So what do you think, Brianne? You ready to try this again between us or are you still running?"

Her feet twitched with the desire to be out the door.

He thought she might be running? If she could find her shoes she'd be sprinting. No matter what tender feelings she'd experienced with Aidan tonight, she didn't have any intention of setting herself up for a fall. Emotions scared her to begin with and the confusing knot of desire, hope and caring she felt for Aidan flat-out terrified her.

"Honestly, I don't know. I'm a little scared." Understatement. "And confused." Even bigger understatement.

"That's allowed. Hell, I don't know what's going on between us either. But I plan on hanging in there until we figure it out."

"I just might need some space to get my head on straight. Between a new business to run, a stepfather on the lam, my mother mixed up in some banking scheme and some loser ex-boyfriend on the loose, I worry about making bad decisions. And I can't think when you're with me."

He shot her a purely male grin—ego-driven and not afraid to show it. "Sometimes thinking is overrated."

Sensation sizzled over her pulse points, bringing to mind moments tonight when she'd submerged herself in feeling.

Resisting the urge to fan herself, she settled for backing up a step. "Remember when I told you I was afraid of reliving my mother's bad choices when it came to men? I made a documentary about dangerous men and the women who love them, and trust me, it's an insidious behavioral pattern I refuse to get trapped in. I've always said I wouldn't follow that same insane road as her and yet I seem to be crossing paths with one dangerous man after another.''

''Don't tell me you're including me in the category with the stalker.'' He thunked a broad hand across his forehead. ''Damn, Brianne. Since when am I the dangerous type?''

''You carry a gun 24/7, don't you? And the scariest part of that is knowing it wouldn't bother me unless I cared about you. A lot.'' Panicking just a little—not that Aidan would ever be dangerous to her, just that she needed to extricate herself from this conversation ASAP—she swept the room with her eyes again. Where the hell were her shoes? ''I just don't think I could handle knowing you were rubbing elbows with criminals, taking risks, putting yourself in danger all the time.''

Call her wimpy. But she'd lose her mind. Maybe it would be different if she could be certain he wouldn't take crazy chances. But she knew Aidan, knew how he felt about his job, and knew he'd put himself on the line at the drop of a hat.

''I know what I'm doing with the gun. Did I mention they don't roll out badges to any slouch with an itch to play cops and robbers?'' Aidan stalked toward the door.

At first she thought he was leaving but then he bent to retrieve something from under the wet bar. Her shoes.

''You seem to be in a damn hurry for these, Brianne, so I'm going to hand them over.'' He delivered them to her, his tall body too close to hers as he dropped them on the floor beside her mocha-almond-painted toenails. "I won't stop you from running and I won't keep you from finding your damn space. But I think you're going to be missing out on something if you don't take a few chances once in a while."

His words tugged at her, made her long to live up to his expectation. "I realize I've been thinking a lot about security these days, not risk. But taking chances certainly proved enjoyable tonight." She smiled up at him as she slid into her strappy shoes. "Would you give me a little longer to try to figure out what I want?"

His nod was curt, but at least he'd agreed. "I'm going to check the status of this guy Vanderwalk now. I'll be down in your office making calls, so just swing by there before you leave or else I can drive you home."

He looked so stern, so serious. She wished she could ease away that stone set of his jaw, but she needed to be true to herself too. "Thanks Aidan. I don't want to sound ungrateful because I really appreciate you helping me out with that."

"Don't be too appreciative because I'm not letting you off the hook on the relationship by a long shot. You're nothing like your mother and I think you're making big-time excuses for your own damn fears by rolling out that one."

He snagged his jacket off the surveillance camera in the corner of the room and headed for the door. "Sooner or later, you've got to stop living life behind a camera lens and see what happens when you step into the real world."

12

FRUSTRATION CHURNED through Aidan as he slouched in Brianne's office chair and punched the phone number for the tenth call on his list. He'd already talked to the cops in New York and Miami Beach, he'd checked up on the whereabouts of James Vanderwalk, and now he followed up on his current investigation.

But throughout the calls he'd been thinking nonstop about his night with Brianne, wondering why the hell their time together had to transform from euphoric to explosive as soon as they'd quit touching and started talking. She needed space? How much damn space could one woman have? She already moved through life like a one-woman island.

Scribbling down notes from his conversation with an agency support staffer on a cocktail napkin he'd found in his pocket, Aidan marveled at the uncluttered black lacquer of Brianne's office desk. She kept exactly one crystal clock, one silver pen and one chrome paperweight on the shiny surface. No paper in sight.

How could he ever communicate with a woman who didn't even reveal a hint of herself on her desk?

In the past, great sex had been a cause for celebration. Now—at 6:00 a.m. according to her crystal clock—he didn't feel much like pounding his chest in he-man victory.

He felt more like pounding the nearest wall.

How could she retreat so fast after the night they'd shared? They'd probably conquered half the positions in the *Kama Sutra*. They definitely must have set some kind of Guinness orgasmic record. But more importantly, she'd felt comfortable enough with him to share pieces of herself, her past.

A feat he suspected didn't come easily to a woman whose office lacked a single photograph or personal memento.

Damn.

But he'd vowed not to tie himself up in knots over any woman, hadn't he? The lesson had been hard-won after his marriage to Natalie, but he'd learned not to get caught up with innocents. And while Brianne wasn't exactly naive, she possessed a depth of vulnerability he hadn't anticipated in someone with such a slick, cool veneer.

He ought to be grateful she was willing to keep their relationship simple. Instead, he had to practically tie himself to her office chair to keep from marching back upstairs to the harem hotel suite and using every persuasive power he possessed to convince her she was making a mistake.

Of course, it didn't help that he could still see her on the wall of security monitors.

Struggling to focus on his phone call, he grew distracted by the image of her on monitor number eight. She hadn't left the harem suite when he did. She'd simply retrieved her laptop from the briefcase she'd carried earlier and plugged into a data port beside the telephone.

Not that he'd been watching her every move or anything.

Scrubbing a palm across tired eyes, Aidan counted himself two times a fool. He needed to pry his gaze off monitor number eight and get his head back to business before he blew this case in a colossal repeat of history. The best thing he could do right now was to follow Brianne's lead and know enough to walk away.

But first, he needed to make one more phone call.

BRIANNE CLICKED THROUGH the keys on her laptop as she lay on the white satin bedspread where she and Aidan had made love. Repeatedly.

Later she would call housekeeping and see about having the room cleaned. Right now, some sadistic part of her reveled in the lingering scent of Aidan's spicy aftershave mingled with her perfume.

Knowing she couldn't go home until Aidan checked the status of her psycho ex-boyfriend, she'd figured hanging out in the harem suite made far more sense than venturing anywhere near her office. Where Aidan would be. So she'd used the time to check out the activity on the bank account in her mother's name.

And managed to discover a few things Aidan would probably want to see.

The phone rang at her bedside, jarring her from her thoughts.

"Hello?"

"Is this enough space for you?" Aidan's husky

tones rumbled across the line, an all-too-familiar voice that made her heart jump.

She smiled in spite of herself. "Depends. Who's calling?"

"This is the Pasha. You know, lord of the harem and all that. I need to speak to my Pasharina."

"We definitely need to do something about the name, don't we? The Pasharina's Palace just isn't cutting it."

"How about the Orgasmic Oasis? Or maybe the Thousand and One Naughty Nights?"

More like Heartbreak Harem, judging from the sorry state of her emotions right now. But she wasn't about to offer that up to Aidan. "The Pasharina is very busy, sir. Is there something I can help you with?"

Brianne heard a half-stifled sigh on the other end of the line and wondered if he felt as frustrated as she did.

"Just wanted to let you know the coast is clear if you want to go home. Vanderwalk is still in New York."

"You found that out already?" She sat upright on the bed, relieved and wary at the same time. How could Aidan be so sure? "What did you do—send the cops to his door?"

There was a moment of silence on the other end. "I called him."

Her jaw dropped. Then, remembering Aidan could see her on the wall of security monitors if he still sat in her office, she snapped it shut again. "You called him?"

"Sometimes the most obvious solution is the best. I

pretended I was a telemarketer and asked him a bunch of nosy questions before he woke up enough to tell me to go to hell. I'm sure it was him.'' In the background she could hear him clicking through the buttons on the foot massager below her desk. He'd obviously discovered her one hidden office indulgence. ''And don't worry, I used a secure line routed from my cell phone. There's no way any caller ID could ever trace it to Florida.''

''You pretended you were a telemarketer?'' This is how the FBI gathered information? Or maybe, that was just how Aidan gathered information. Unorthodox, but impressive nevertheless. ''Is that legal?''

''Put it this way, it's a hell of a lot more legal than stalking.''

He had her there. ''You're right. And I would have given my eyeteeth to have those cops in New York gather that much intelligence on Jimmy while I lived there.'' She glanced up at the camera for his benefit, wanting him to know how much his effort meant to her. ''Thank you. I'm going to sleep better at night now.''

''I'd still be careful, Brianne. I'm going to check in with the police in New York every now and then, but if your security needs any beefing up at home, you'll want to invest the time on it.'' The note of concern in his voice warmed her. Made her feel protected in a way she'd never been before.

''I found out a few things for you, too,'' she blurted, unwilling to sort through the swirl of emotions Aidan inspired in her. She swiveled her laptop to face the security camera. ''If you want a close-up of the screen, just click on the number eight button on my master control remote and press the zoom key.''

"Got it. I'm zooming. What do you have there? On-line banking statements?''

"They're for the bogus account in my mother's name.''

He whistled long and low under his breath. "You don't access those by pretending you're a telemarketer. Care to tell me how you managed that?''

"By operating under the assumption Mel set up the account. I tried out Melvin-style passwords and finally got through with 'Go Marlins.' All caps. But then, Melvin's whole lifestyle had been about over-enthusiasm, hearty laughter and too much money.'' She pointed to the screen. "These are recent transactions. As you can see, he had several large influxes of cash shortly before he made off with the resort's entire operating budget.''

"Holy shit. You mean I can go pull up that whole account if I type in Go Marlins? That's damn brilliant.''

"The words run together and they have to be in all caps. And you need to know my mother's maiden name at one point. It's McCormick.'' A surge of pride swelled through her at his compliment, but she felt compelled to point out she only possessed the skill because she'd never been the type to step into the spotlight. "And it's not *brilliant*—it's just *me*. I've probably spent as much time behind a computer screen as I have behind a camera. When you grow up in a tumultuous environment, you learn to appreciate scenarios that provide you with a little anonymity. And a little space.''

He could take that however he wanted, but damn it, he needed to know.

Finally, his voice rumbled back over the line. "I can practically see you drawing your line in the sand.''

"It's not a line, Aidan. It's a simple fact of who I am.''

"I'm too tired to make intelligent arguments this morning. Now that you've uncovered this bit of news I've got my work cut out for me for the next twenty-four hours. I probably won't be at the club until late, but I'll be there.'' He huffed out a sigh. "I've got a few ideas on where to look for the source of this influx of cash.''

They stumbled through awkward good-nights. Brianne had prepped her response in case Aidan offered to drive her home. Like a first-class hypocrite, she couldn't deny a twinge of disappointment when the offer never came. Apparently Aidan seemed to have decided he wouldn't push her on the space issue.

Which was what she wanted. Right?

Still, she couldn't deny her sense of disappointment as their tenuous connection cracked a little more when he hung up the phone.

BRIANNE ARRIVED at the club shortly before sunset the next day and nearly tripped over Summer hunched near the floor in the corridor.

"Sorry!'' Summer straightened, still holding a chunk of ceramic tile in one hand, a heavy tool belt hanging around her hips. "Lainie said we don't have the budget to redo the whole floor to the spa so I'm just scattering a random pattern of tiles I like better among the old ones to spruce it up a bit.'' She moved aside so Brianne could see the sandy-color tiles mixed in with the solid red terra-cotta. ''I'd better pick up now that you're here though. Giselle wants us all to meet at eight-thirty before opening tonight.''

''The new tiles look great, Summer.'' The woman might be unconventional in a lot of ways but she had an amazing eye for design. ''Will we be in the conference room?''

''Are you kidding?'' She scooped up a small pot of some sticky substance and a small stack of tiles. ''I'm hoping we'll *never* have to meet in the conference room. See you at the hot tub!''

With a wink and a grin, Summer sashayed away in her pinstriped overalls and pink paisley tank top.

Leaving Brianne to scramble for a swimsuit so she could make the hot tub appointment. She'd hardly slept the night before. The morning before, rather. She hadn't gotten home until 8:00 a.m. and then she'd been too busy thinking about Aidan to sleep.

She'd finally given up trying at noon and had worked on her master control remote for the house instead. So far she'd incorporated the security controls, the house intercom system, her sprinkler system and the chandelier-lowering device into the remote. Tomorrow she'd work on adding her alarm clock and all the timed devices—coffeepot, dishwasher, dryer and so on.

But the technical work that had been her safe haven in the past hadn't provided the usual comforts.

Thoughts of Aidan still slipped through her guard, causing her to make beginner mistakes. She'd forgotten to give the sprinklers an override shutoff switch and then she'd set the chandelier to raise and lower much too quickly.

Still, she preferred spending a sleepless night thanks to sensual memories of Aidan than spending a sleepless night scared her ex would show up on her doorstep. And for that added security, Brianne counted herself truly grateful.

Tossing a hotel robe around her shoulders she made her way to the hot tub for the meeting. As she levered open the tinted door to go outside she spied Giselle and Summer already neck high in bubbles and engaged in a squirt gun battle.

Behind Brianne, a pair of high heels picked up speed.

"Hold that door." Lainie wore an elegant silk caftan bearing a fire-breathing dragon and toted an over-stuffed briefcase. She stepped through the smoked glass then sighed as her gaze landed on the water fight in progress. "I could stand her sleeping with my husband, Brianne, but if she splashes me I can no longer be responsible for my actions."

Brianne didn't need to ask who *she* was. Poor Giselle still hadn't found a way to heal her rift with Lainie.

"I think I'll be able to make them hold their fire." Brianne whispered the words as they neared the hot tub. Not that their squealing partners would have heard them over the roar of the bubble jets and their own laughter. "You realize she had absolutely no idea that Robert was married at the time, don't you?"

She had never considered herself much of a friend in the pseudo-counselor, advice-dispensing department, but the rift between Giselle and Lainie had the power to wreak havoc in their four-way partnership if they couldn't solve their problems.

Lainie dropped her briefcase on to a beach lounger with a thud and Brianne thought she might have seen the other woman bite her lip. But then, Lainie faced her again, her eyes as fierce as the dragon's on her robe. "On my charitable days—yes. While PMSing, however, I tend to forget. Feel free to muzzle me if you see any fangs start to sprout."

"Got it." Brianne waded into the fray in the small pool and disarmed both combatants, but not before sneaking in two squirts for each of them with her confiscated weapons. "All clear, Lainie. I think it's safe."

With that, Lainie cruised into her lawyer manner to run the meeting from a built-in lounger seat in the hot tub. While the waves rolled a steady thrum on to the beach behind the resort, they watched the stars come out overhead and waded through new business under a waning Libra moon. At least that's what Summer assured them.

The group approved several new decorating themes, reviewed their first few nights' operating expenses on spreadsheets conveniently tucked into plastic protectors, and confirmed their reopening for at least a portion of the hotel in two weeks' time. The redecorating effort would continue for months but they needed the income of renting rooms out to support further updates in the resort.

As they finished business and poured the champagne—a must for keeping spirits up in a new venture, they all agreed—Giselle proposed a toast to their success. "And although I tried to tell my family I didn't need their help," Giselle continued between sips, "my brothers said they will be stopping by the club in the next couple of weeks. So if anyone stumbles on a bunch of Italian guys who look like Mafia dropouts, don't panic—the Cesare brothers have arrived. You can just point them toward the kitchen and I'll try to keep them out of the way."

Summer clinked her glass against Brianne's. "Woohoo! Just what we need. More men."

"Speaking of which," Brianne settled deeper into her neck massager seat and let the jets soothe some of the edgy tension away that had been dogging her ever since Aidan showed up at Club Paradise. "Anything new to report in the men department?"

She was much better at asking the questions than being on the receiving end so why not beat them to the punch?

Lainie rolled her eyes, Giselle shook her head full of pinned-up dark hair and Summer snorted. "Any guys I've talked to here are either too wild or as interesting as cardboard. Nothing in between."

"Amen." Giselle obviously seconded the notion.

"What about you, Brianne?" Lainie posed the question with her attorney in cross-examination mode voice—friendly enough on the surface, but probably ready to pounce. "Is Agent Maddock still determined to be your lover?"

Brianne nearly choked on her sparkling bubbles. "Excuse me?"

"I thought our FBI friend planned to manufacture an affair with you as a cover for his presence in the club," Lainie replied easily while Giselle and Summer smothered laughter. "But I guess no one has seen enough of him for him to need a cover. Except for you, of course."

Brianne had the sinking feeling the cat had leapt out of the bag. In a hurry. "I take it I'm caught?"

"The girls in housekeeping were suspicious that they were getting laundry orders before we opened for business," Summer supplied helpfully once she got her smirk under control. "I don't think any of us are going to be able to keep secrets around here."

Brianne floundered for how to respond to conversation she would categorize as girl talk. Something she'd done an excellent job of sidestepping up until now in her life. "Unfortunately our attraction makes no sense."

"That's the best kind!" Giselle protested, topping off the champagne Brianne had gulped down in a hurry. "I think that's totally romantic."

Brianne failed to see what could be romantic about falling for a guy who carried a gun and spent his nights in raucous clubs, his days in the most dangerous parts of town.

Although she couldn't deny she'd been a little weak-kneed when she'd discovered the big, bad-ass federal agent had pretended to be a telemarketer to make sure her psycho ex-boyfriend was still far away.

"Just don't toss aside a chance for happiness because Maddock doesn't fit your idea of the right guy for you, Bri." Summer added her wisdom to the pile while Brianne waited to hear Lainie's verdict on the situation.

And waited.

"Call me Machiavellian," Lainie finally began, tapping one shiny red nail on the smooth concrete rim of the sunken hot tub. "But I just keep thinking how cool it would be for one of our partners to have an 'in' with the FBI. Voila—instant credibility again. I'm thinking it would be a sound corporate investment for us to spring for the wedding."

"A wedding?" Brianne didn't waste any time reaching for the confiscated squirt gun and letting Lainie have it—red nails, perfect hair and all.

And as the Club Paradise management meeting erupted into a full-scale water war, Brianne couldn't help but think she'd done pretty well at her first foray into girl talk.

She just hoped her diversionary tactic of a squirt gun battle had concealed the fluttery panic attack that had accompanied Lainie's mention of Aidan and a wedding.

And she really, really hoped that the fluttering feeling she'd experienced had indeed been a panic attack, and not—as some inner voice kept insisting—a little bit of hope.

13

AIDAN SHOULDERED his way out the back doors of the Moulin Rouge Lounge toward the patio late that night. Stepping on to the sprawling deck behind the club, he took deep breaths of the fresh ocean breeze blowing off the water, a welcome respite after the smoke-filled labyrinth of the A-list hot spot he'd just left.

Would this be enough space for Brianne?

Him outside, her ensconced in her office a few hundred yards away through concrete and steel. She seemed most at home in her sterile, high-tech world without messy complications—where she held all the controls.

In charge. Alone.

He walked away from the club, through the expanse of deck loungers and patio tables and toward the water to meet his contact. Tonight's earlier appointment with Daisy had come up empty. The club's cigarette girl had been more interested in romance than relaying information so Aidan had cut ties with her. He wondered if Brianne had realized that from her office perch on the other side of the camera that had no doubt witnessed the incident.

Did she understand Aidan had been freeing her from

her services, or did she only see Daisy's ever-ready kisses?

A man could only escape an anaconda so quickly.

Feet zigzagging in and out of the surf, Aidan dared the water to touch his shoes while he looked for his next contact and thought about Brianne.

The meeting with Daisy tonight might have been professionally frustrating, but it had also been personally enlightening. Those few seconds of being accosted by a relentless female had made him realize he didn't want to waste any more time in his life hanging out with women only interested on the most basic of human connection.

Sex in South Beach was pretty damn easy to come by after all. He hadn't exactly been deprived in that department since his divorce.

Being groped by the overenthusiastic Daisy helped him see he'd reached a point in life where he wanted more than sex. And he wanted *more* with Brianne Wolcott.

But first he needed to convince her to give up a little of that space she seemed too intent on keeping.

He'd covered about a quarter of a mile before his feet got wet. Funny how thinking about Brianne had the power to shatter his focus every time.

"Aidan?" The masculine voice of his new contact carried through the dark on the wind.

Turning, Aidan spotted Jackson Taggart reclining on a low-slung lounger amid a grouping of resort chairs left on the beach. Jackson sported a golf shirt and jeans—not his usual jacket and tie getup. His short hair stood on end as if he'd run restless fingers through it more than once.

Lowering himself into a seat beside his rumpled college roommate, Aidan settled back against the weathered canvas to stare out over the waves. "Sorry I couldn't meet you any earlier. I'm finding myself with several leads all of a sudden and a lot to follow up on." Not to mention Brianne's close encounter with a stalker.

He'd taken time away from his investigation this afternoon to cash in favors with every agent he knew in and around New York. If Vanderwalk took a flight out of the city or used his credit card to purchase gas in another state, Aidan planned to know about it.

Jackson nodded, only half listening. His gaze swept the dark water as if searching for a horizon he wouldn't find for hours. "No problem. I just wanted to let you know I have reason to believe Melvin Baxter is on the move. Probably within Florida state lines. Possibly in the city."

Aidan thought the same thing. But he knew damn well Jackson would never make a statement without proof. "I'm really hoping you're not going to cop out on how you heard this by offering up some bogus attorney-client privilege."

He held his breath while he waited for an answer.

The response could make or break his case.

Finally, Jackson shook his head. "It's nothing like that. I'd never betray a confidence that way. This is a hell of a lot more esoteric. I don't have a clue if I'm doing the right thing by coming to you."

Shoving up to a sitting position, Aidan confronted

his longtime friend. "You're a grade A straight arrow. What choice would you have besides coming to the FBI if you had information pertaining to the case?"

"I overheard my father talking to Mel on the phone tonight."

His father the former FBI director. His father the popular politician and reigning head of the sprawling Taggart clan. His father the betrayer whom Aidan had come to suspect of thwarting his first case ten years ago.

"Shit." Aidan knew that had to suck. He'd been avoiding a conversation with Jackson about his dad for weeks because nobody wanted to hear their parent might be operating on the wrong side of the law.

"My thoughts exactly." Jackson met his eyes in the dim light cast by a long line of resorts built on the water. "I went by my parents' place for dinner tonight and ended up catching snippets of my dad's call while he was talking on a phone in the garden. I should have walked away. Or else I should have confronted him about it afterward." He scrubbed a hand across his forehead and back over his scalp, causing his close-cut hair to stand up even straighter. "But the whole thing reeks of bad news and I didn't know who else to call."

The time had arrived for Aidan to be honest about his suspicions of the elder Taggart. Jackson deserved to know everything Aidan could tell him—which sure as hell wasn't much—but he damn well wouldn't like it.

First, Aidan needed to cut through the personal ramifications of the situation to figure out what Mel was up to, however. "What exactly went down during this conversation?"

"Hearing only one side of it, I can't know for sure. But it sounded to me like Mel was asking my dad to move money around for him." Jackson huffed out a sigh. Drummed his fingers on the polished wooden armrests of his lounge chair. "Possibly he only called to ask my father to represent him, but that seems unlikely since Dad hasn't practiced criminal defense in almost twenty years. He would never consider taking on a high-profile case with such a well-known crook, especially as he's up for a judge's seat if the fall elections go his way."

Of course they hadn't been discussing that. Mel hadn't even been arrested yet. He sure as hell wouldn't be shopping for an attorney.

And Aidan had a new reason to face old man Taggart with his accusations. No way would he stand by while Jackson's father was appointed to the judge's bench if the guy had conspired with criminals in his past.

"What makes you think Mel needed him to move money around?" Aidan liked to think Melvin sat in a hotel somewhere under an anonymous name, growing more and more nervous about his U.S. bank accounts.

Growing more and more nervous that Aidan breathed down his neck.

Jackson quit his drumming rhythm. "Dad said something about banks needing extensive identification to withdraw that much money."

Bingo.

And if Mel begged a favor from a prominent Miami

politician when he needed to remain underground, he must be getting desperate for his cash. Now that Taggart had said no, Aidan had a good idea who would be next on Mel's list.

Too bad Aidan would talk to her first.

Before Aidan could comment, Jackson pounded the armrest with his fist. "If Dad had some sort of long-ago attorney-client relationship with Melvin and I'm breaking that confidence by talking to you—"

"He couldn't have and you know it." Aidan wouldn't let Jack beat himself up over this. He was too honorable of a guy to be caught up in crooked politics. "Your father could have never supervised my investigation into the Baxter case ten years ago when he was a director at the Bureau if he'd ever worked with Melvin."

A string of curses unlike anything Aidan had ever heard issued forth from Jack's mouth. And that was saying something considering some of the bad-ass trash talkers Aidan had tangled with in his day.

Then Jackson's shoulders slumped, yet his body remained taut with a tension Aidan couldn't begin to imagine. He knew he needed to hash this out with Jackson tonight, he just hoped he'd have enough time left to face Brianne before she hotfooted out of the club. He'd given her some space, but he'd be damned if he'd back off.

Aidan glanced back up at Club Paradise and wondered if Brianne had thought about him half as much today as he'd thought about her. About what they'd shared.

Yeah, he definitely needed to talk to her about last

night. But first, the time had come for him and Jack to have a long conversation. "I've been meaning to talk to you about your father...."

BRIANNE'S FINGER HOVERED over the rewind button for camera number seven. If she nudged the surveillance tape back by just a few hours she'd be able to see Aidan fending off some major tongue work from Daisy the cigarette girl.

Again.

Tapping the key, she reminded herself she didn't want to watch any such thing. Bad enough she'd had to view them together—again—on live video feed earlier that night. Yet some inner demon kept reminding her of their odd interaction, urged her to roll the tape one more time so she could tell herself Aidan was a player.

That he would never be the man for her.

Her finger twitched, wriggled. Then finally stabbed the stop button with resounding force.

No way would she play adolescent games with herself. Or Aidan. They both deserved better from her, especially since she recognized Aidan had ended whatever relationship he'd had with Daisy. Body language told a more eloquent story than words ever could. And judging by Aidan's tense reaction to Daisy's lascivious lips, Brianne knew the petite blonde hadn't exactly been lighting his fire.

Brianne just hoped she'd have the chance to try sparking a few flames with him again one of these days.

Sighing, she shut down the club for the night, locking doors and tightening security with the flip of a few switches. Aidan hadn't returned since early that night when their exchange had been stiff, cool.

She'd been so busy chewing nails over the whole Daisy incident she hadn't bothered to think it through rationally, let alone ask Aidan about it. Instead she'd retreated behind her safe walls and Aidan hadn't seemed to mind giving her the space. He'd been distracted, edgy to leave the office.

And she hadn't seen him—on camera or off—since then.

The empty ache inside her all night told her she missed him. She had no idea how his case had progressed in the last twenty-four hours because she hadn't bothered to ask him in her haste to run away.

Not only was she intellectually curious about his investigation, she realized she cared about it because he did.

All signs pointed to her falling for him hard and fast despite her lame attempts to keep him at arm's length. Maybe instead of pushing Aidan away because of her insecurities, she should be tackling her own problems in the hope that one day she'd be ready for the kind of relationship he seemed to offer.

The notion frightened and excited her at the same time. And as she wondered how she could ever get her act together enough to be with an FBI agent for more than just one night, a knock sounded at her office door.

Just as Aidan stepped into the room.

A thrill jumped through her at the sight of him. A tangible, head-to-toe current that tingled over her nerves, whispered across her skin and snaked along the hem of her sleek gray minidress.

"Hi." She stood in the middle of her office with the lights already dimmed for the night. Only her monitors blinked on the wall behind her. Her greeting seemed inadequate for all that she'd been thinking and feeling about him in the last few hours, but one look at him had scattered her thoughts.

Rendered her breathless.

He locked the door behind him. Behind them.

"I'm not leaving." He announced this with arms folded. Between the stance of his body and the black Harley T-shirt cut off at the shoulders, he looked like a Hells Angel guarding the backstage door at a Rolling Stones concert.

Okay, maybe not quite that intimidating. Despite his resolute posture, she did have the security of knowing she could make at least *one* part of this man move.

"Oh, really?" She leaned back on the edge of her desk, relishing his proximity with her whole body while she ate up his presence with her eyes.

"I don't know what the hell I was thinking letting you scare me off with the old 'I need space' routine, but I've had time to think it over and I've got news for you, lady." He stared her down with glittering gray eyes. He looked like a man who had tangled with danger and lived to tell about it. A man who could hold his own no matter what came his way.

"And that is?" Her heart pounded faster. Harder.

"It's bullshit." He relaxed his stance, walked toward her. Closer. Closer. "Pure, undiluted, smoke-screen bullshit."

Despite the fact that she'd reached a similar conclusion herself, Brianne couldn't help a shade of defensiveness. Or maybe it had more to do with some stray desire to see how far Aidan would take the offensive. "I don't know about that. I shared with you as much as I understood myself."

Electric emotion crackled between them, heated the very air around them.

"Then you weren't trying too hard." His hands reached out for her, skimmed her waist through the cotton jersey fabric of her short dress. "In fact, I think all your talk about needing space was just another way of saying you were too scared to try something real with me."

"I'm not scared now." Okay, maybe she was a little scared, but not enough to make her turn away. She wanted nothing more than to wrap her arms around him. To soak up his strength, his warmth that she'd been missing all night.

"That's because you're simmering with the same heat that's firing me up inside." His hands smoothed a path up her sides until his thumbs grazed the underside of her breasts. Sent a jolt of desire straight to her most secret places. "Tomorrow you'll scram for that door so fast I'd have to tie you down to keep you here. Although, come to think of it…" He seemed to weigh the merit of the idea.

"No more running." The certainty in her voice sprang from some place deep inside her. Some secret well of her soul she hadn't known existed. She might not know how they would work around her fear of his job once their feet hit the floor, but she knew damn well she intended to try.

His eyes darkened at her words, his gaze narrowing a split second before he leaned closer. "No more running."

If Aidan planned to issue the words as a command, they lost some of their intimidation in his husky, whispered delivery. But they didn't lose their power to sway her.

Brianne melted into him as Aidan's palms cupped her breasts, squeezed her gently between his hands as he caught her lips to his for a kiss. He tasted like the ocean, clean and salty. She clung to his arms for fear she'd drown in him. Whereas other kisses they'd shared had been about a seesaw battle for control, this kiss was all about surrender.

His. Hers.

Theirs.

Brianne's knees weakened with it, allowing Aidan to draw her down to the floor with him. She lay on the new carpet, welcomed the warmth of Aidan's tall body stretched over top of her. Heedless of their surroundings, she didn't care that her office lacked the sensual appeal of the harem or the urgency factor of making love on her desktop.

She could have been anywhere and it wouldn't have mattered. Her interest lay solely in this man and not in any extraneous trappings of silk or satin.

She wanted *him*. Aidan Maddock.

And she'd gladly stretch out on the floor of the office for the chance to feel his body against her, the chance to welcome him inside her.

Aidan's hands cupped her face, combed through her hair, delved into the neckline of her dress. His fingers lacked the teasing skill of their other couplings. Tonight his touch possessed an awkwardness, a needy possessiveness that she felt too.

Together they managed to discard Aidan's trousers, his briefs. Aidan didn't bother removing her dress, settling instead for peeling away her panties and lifting her hem.

He'd found a condom from somewhere—bless him—and he was prepared to protect her even here, on the floor of her office.

She loved that about him. That nobility, the steadfast sense of honor that ran through his veins despite his unconventional ways. No backwards baseball cap or cut-off Harley shirt could disguise the upstanding principles that had attracted her to him from the first time they'd met.

All traces of awkwardness disappeared when Aidan's hands pressed against her thighs to nudge her legs wider. She stared up at him above her and read the intent in his eyes.

Simple. Primal.

Immediate.

She barely had time to process the import of that moment, the subtle warning they were crossing a line, when he lowered himself to his elbows and brought them nose-to-nose.

The heady heat of his body notched up her own temperature by another couple of degrees. The sea-blown scent of him made her want to bury her nose in his shoulder, taste and explore every inch of him.

He edged himself inside her as his tongue lay claim to her mouth. The possession was swift and total and Brianne clung to him with all her strength.

Other times when they'd made love she had held a part of herself back, some deep-seated sense of self she had never been willing to share with anyone. But now she allowed herself to let go, to give everything she had to this moment, this man.

The risk of losing herself loomed, yet she refused to let fear rule her. Refused to run away.

As his lips trailed kisses down her neck and called up shivers all over her skin, Brianne vowed tonight she would claim Aidan every bit as much as he claimed her.

Aidan nipped and tasted Brianne's soft flesh as his fingers flexed into the low pile carpet beneath them. He prayed for some last vestige of restraint to rein him in before he slid under the seductive spell of Brianne totally. Completely.

Never to surface again.

Her body clenched around his as sweat popped out along his brow. Struggling to hold himself back for just a little longer, he knew damn well his release this time would leave all other experiences in the dust.

He'd had better control last night in the harem hotel room when he'd been underneath Brianne and at her mercy. But then, that time had been all about doling out sensual experiences and seeing who could still walk away at the end without turning bow-legged.

Tonight didn't have a damn thing to do with sex or sensuality or playing provocative games. From the moment he'd kissed Brianne, this night had been all about surrender.

His pending, hers already given in the most humbling moment of his life. Somehow he got more than he bargained for in pushing her.

One minute he'd been lying over her, dying to taste her, needing to be inside her. And the next minute she'd given him everything he'd wanted and more, opened herself to him in a way no woman had.

Not even his wife.

This was different. Bigger. Scarier.

Her breathy moans in his ear called him to join her as her nails grazed his back. Some sane portion of his brain told him he'd be crossing a point of no return, but his every instinct strained to surrender right back. To lose himself in her as totally as she'd lost herself in him.

He hadn't undressed her all the way, hadn't taken her to new heights of pleasure, hadn't touched her with a lover's skill. Instead he'd been too hungry simply to *join* them. Bond them.

Even as the import of that daunting realization washed over him, he was powerless to find that damned elusive last remnant of control.

Brianne wriggled and nudged, kissed and licked him. She closed her eyes and wrapped herself more tightly around him, a feat he wouldn't have thought possible two seconds prior. Her nails dug lightly into his shoulder and he knew the little crescent moon marks would remain there tomorrow.

And still those tender jabs weren't nearly enough to haul him back to sanity.

Knowing he didn't have a choice, hoping he could make it up to her later, he simply shifted between her thighs and buried himself all the deeper.

As his hoarse shout mingled with Brianne's, Aidan knew his surrender had been every bit as complete as hers.

FEAR SET IN as the morning light filtered through the blinds in Brianne's office to tickle Aidan's eyelids. After they'd made love a second time—and a third—he'd slept fitfully for an hour or so on the floor beside her.

He'd told himself over and over that he'd be able to handle the reality of a relationship between them. He'd pursued it, pursued her even when she'd asked him for distance. After all, he'd been married before. And while that relationship had exploded in his face, it hadn't soured him on the idea of commitment.

Except what he and Brianne had experienced hadn't felt like simple commitment. No, they'd touched something bigger and—though it made him realize what a crappy husband he'd been to Natalie—more important.

Staring down at Brianne cradled in the crook of his arm, he realized two things. First, he'd underestimated her power to get under his skin. Second, he'd overestimated his ability to handle his feelings for her.

Not that he couldn't handle it, necessarily.

He just decided Brianne's idea of a little distance hadn't been such a bad idea. It had probably been a fantastic idea, he'd simply been too determined to have his own way to realize it.

Reaching down to stroke her face, Aidan smoothed an errant lock of auburn hair trailing over her cheek.

Tenderness for this woman stole through him even as he realized he couldn't stay here with her. Not now. Not today.

As the morning light called to him, urged him to get a move on, he told himself that he simply needed to return to his case. Shoving to his feet, he moved carefully around Brianne, not wanting to wake her. Not ready to talk to her just yet.

Gently he scooped her off the floor and lay her on the leather couch in her office. Her brow furrowed as he moved away from her but she didn't waken.

As he penned her a note he explained that he was at a crucial point in the investigation. That much was the truth. He couldn't afford to remain with Brianne while Melvin plotted his next move.

But deep inside he acknowledged his own relief at having the safe out. Because no matter how much he'd told himself he could handle the next step between him and Brianne, the reality of taking their relationship to the next level in the wake of last night had him second-guessing himself.

He'd screwed up his marriage and although the regret and the sense of loss had torn him up, he'd managed to move on and reconstruct his life. Stay positive.

If he committed himself to Brianne, the tough-as-nails firecracker who had surrendered herself to him on every level, he knew the stakes would be a hell of a lot higher.

The cost to his heart might be more than he could risk.

14

SO SHE HADN'T BEEN showered with roses the morning after her surrender of heart, body and soul to Aidan. So what?

Prowling around the bedroom of her Palm Beach house the next day, Brianne punched a fist through each armhole of the slim black sheath dress she'd chosen for her meeting with her mother. She assured herself there were worse ways to wake up than with a note shoved between the office couch cushions.

Offhand, she couldn't think of any.

But surely if she quizzed her partners in Club Paradise they could think of a scenario or two. Lainie alone could probably supply her with enough morning-after horror stories to make her feel grateful Aidan at least left a note.

He'd written something about needing to work on his investigation today and she could buy that. What she failed to understand as she rummaged through her closet for just the right shoes was why he had to leave without telling her face-to-face.

And he had accused *her* of being scared?

Hah! At least she'd stuck around long enough to tell him she'd been scared. Aidan had probably left tire tracks on Ocean Drive in his haste to run at the first sign of deep emotion.

No matter. Slipping into a pair of funky black mules with tiny silver studs on the heels, Brianne figured if his fears about a relationship between them were anything like hers, they'd be temporary. Surmountable.

Or so she hoped.

If his concerns ran deeper than that, she might have chased him away by allowing him to glimpse a bit of her heart last night. She'd be hurt, but she wouldn't let that sway her from her course.

Spritzing herself with a tiny shot from her perfume bottle, she rushed around the bedroom picking up strewn clothes and trying to restore a little order to a life—and house—gone haywire. Regardless of how Aidan felt, she needed to get her act together, starting today. She'd been wary of men long before Jimmy Vanderwalk and the ensuing harassment, but she'd allowed her experience with him to push her even farther behind the safe walls of her high-tech world. She'd made it such a mission to keep herself secure, to control her world in spite of a man who wanted to invade it with phone calls and poems and threats. Aidan's suggestion that she try life in the real world had made her realize how far she'd retreated.

But as of today, there would be no more hiding behind her camera lens or a computer screen. No more hiding behind her glasses when she went to Pauline's house.

She purposely left the velvet case containing the black frames on her nightstand as she headed for the door.

Later, she would think about Aidan. For now as she drove the few blocks down the palm-tree-lined streets that separated her house from her mother's, she planned to concentrate on overcoming a few fears of her own. Before she could ever get involved with any man, she needed to make an effort to talk to Pauline. First she had to assure herself she wasn't turning into her mother, and then—with any luck—she needed to convince Pauline to quit hanging out with dangerous guys.

Maybe they could enter their own twelve-step program together. Because as much as she wanted Aidan, she also knew his job would make her insane. Scare her into thinking up frightening new scenarios for how he might get hurt while chasing bad guys.

As she sat at a stoplight, Brianne allowed her head to drop on to the steering wheel of the sleek black Lexus she'd bought for herself when she'd left New York. She knocked her forehead against the cushioned leather twice before the light turned green.

One thing at a time, she counseled herself, wishing she could remember some of the wisdom from the documentary she'd made about dangerous men and the women who love them. First, she'd worry about her own issues, then she'd figure out what to do about Aidan.

As she turned down her mother's street and spied Aidan's car parked two doors down from Pauline's house, however, Brianne realized she would have to confront that issue sooner than she'd thought.

Because the dangerous man she'd been in the process of falling for was apparently making visits to her mother on the sly.

He was already out of his car and headed for Pauline's as Brianne drove closer, his tall, muscular body and dark good looks a sight to behold even when she was miffed. No, make that angry.

Hadn't it occurred to him to mention in his note that while he was working on his case it just so happened that he'd be hanging out at her mother's house today? She parked the Lexus right behind his Ford and hopped out of the sedan, her high heels tapping in double time on the suburban sidewalk as she caught up with him.

Aidan turned, his body swiveling enough to give her a quick glimpse of the gun tucked into his waistband underneath his suit jacket. He had the FBI-guy look down to a T between the blue suit and the shades. Only the narrowly trimmed beard and mustache detracted from the image.

"You can't be here." He shook his head, his fists clenching and unclenching at his sides.

"Well, that's a mighty fine greeting, lover." She realized she was scrambling behind comfortable defenses by shooting off that attitude. But damn it, his reaction hurt.

Hadn't last night touched him at all?

"I'm serious, Brianne. You need to get in the car and drive away." The smooth, unwavering tone of his voice put her on guard.

"Is my mother in danger?" When his response didn't come immediately, she felt the punch of fear clear to her toes. "I'm not leaving if she might be in trouble."

"She's not in trouble." He looked back up at Pauline's house over one shoulder. "But having you here will only complicate things."

"You think I have a *choice* about walking away now? Welcome to the world of deep emotions, Aidan. You might fight them, but I'm not going to anymore." She planted her feet on the concrete and mentally dared him to shove her aside. "She's my mother and I'm not leaving."

Pauline might have her idiosyncrasies, but she'd done her best to be a good mother. Brianne wouldn't let her get ensnared in some mysterious FBI operation without a little backup. Her mother would probably evade all the questions that struck her as too blunt and end up arrested for obstructing justice.

She watched Aidan's jaw tighten and wished she could see behind those dark sunglasses to his eyes. Didn't he realize he'd have to tie her to the streetlamp to make her stay put when her mother could be in trouble? Not wanting to give him any ideas, she kept the information to herself.

Aidan knew he couldn't take the time to deal with Brianne right now and he couldn't afford a big scene. He could see by the expression on her face, the stubborn tilt of her chin that he'd have a major battle on his hands if he tried to keep her away anyhow.

And valuable time ticked by while they debated the issue.

"Fine. But you follow my lead. Stay back. And run like hell if I tell you to." He didn't anticipate trouble. Brianne and Pauline should be long gone by the time Mel put in an appearance—if he showed up at all. Actually crossing paths with one of Florida's Most Wanted here in a quiet, upscale Palm Beach neighborhood was a long shot, but Aidan refused to take chances.

He waited until she nodded, then resumed his trek up the sidewalk toward her mother's house and the cluster of artsy topiary bushes in a potted grouping around the front door. Ever since Jackson told him Mel actively sought someone to move his money around, Aidan had been concerned about Pauline.

The most logical choice of people to make the big withdrawal Mel needed would be the person whose name appeared on all the paperwork—Pauline Wolcott-Baxter-and-so-on. Mel had never resorted to crimes that involved physically hurting other people before, but desperate men could be unpredictable.

For that reason, Aidan knocked on the door while he kept Brianne behind him. When Pauline didn't answer the second time, Brianne reached around him to try the door herself.

Her long, lean body grazed his as she stretched, reminding him of how much they'd shared last night. Positive this wasn't the time for those kinds of thoughts, Aidan ruthlessly shoved them to the back of his mind while she nudged the door open.

"That is definitely not following protocol," Aidan whispered over his shoulder. "I've got rules to follow for these kinds of situations, Brianne."

"This is my mother's house," she whispered back. "I'm going in now because you've got me worried. And don't try to pretend you're Mr. By the Rules at this late stage of the game. I know you too damn well for that.''

She had him there. But then, he wouldn't have allowed Brianne within a mile of him today if he'd been following procedure to the letter. Her presence on today's investigative efforts marked the biggest bending of the rules so far.

Damn.

He didn't like this one bit. Where was Pauline?

Ruthlessly shoving Brianne further behind him he edged his way into her mother's house. Slowly. Carefully.

All the while he padded with silent feet into the foyer he told himself this investigation would not go up in flames like his last bout with Melvin Baxter. He knew what he was doing now. And any rule-breaking he engaged in happened only because he'd grown experienced enough to know when and how to ignore the rules.

He sure as hell wouldn't make a rookie mistake like allowing his feelings for a woman to cloud his judgment, would he?

As he rounded the corner of the foyer to peer down the hall, he found nothing. No one.

He sensed more than heard Brianne's breathing picking up pace behind him. Turning to meet her gaze, he told her silently to stay put. Miraculously, she did what he wanted, freeing him to search the house with quick, silent efficiency.

Nothing.

As he wound around the silver teacart that still stood

in the middle of the parlor back toward Brianne, he noticed she wasn't where he'd left her.

Shit.

Fear iced through him as his feet picked up speed.

He'd never forgive himself if anything happened to her because he hadn't been able to tell her no—

And then there she was. Poised at the threshold of French doors lining the back of the dining room. Staring out over her mother's garden.

Her eyes cut to his, her wide green gaze full of surprise, maybe a hint of fear. He joined her at the window to see what had caught her attention, determined nothing would frighten her for so much as a second as long as he was around.

Sliding into place in front of her—ready to protect her from anything, be it a garter snake or one of Melvin's lackey crook friends—Aidan found Pauline.

Engaged in a lip lock hot enough to generate sparks, Pauline was barely visible from the man who seemed determined to perform a tonsillectomy then and there.

Although the guy's face was partly obstructed from view thanks to an overgrown hibiscus plant, there were only so many men in the state of Florida who wore a three-piece seersucker suit with a Panama hat and a gold watch large enough to give Big Ben a run for the money.

Melvin Baxter.

Aidan wanted to cheer himself hoarse at his good luck. If only Brianne weren't smack dab in the middle of the upcoming arrest.

''Stay here.'' He mouthed the words even though a pane of leaded glass separated them from the estranged couple who appeared to be settling their differences in record time. "Your mother will be fine."

Easy for him to say, Brianne thought as her heart pounded with a mixture of fear and dread. She stared back at him in the obnoxiously cheery sunlight of Florida at high noon, knowing her mother was about to come face-to-face with one of the most blunt, unhappy truths of her life.

She wanted to tell Aidan something. Be kind. Be careful. But he was already slipping out the door and out of her reach, entering a world of danger she'd never understand.

Sunlight glinted off the polished steel in his right palm as he sprinted over the lawn and vaulted a row of foxgloves.

His gun.

The knot of fear that had started the moment she saw her mother kissing Melvin tightened into a sharp ache of pain centered in her chest. She ached for her mother. For Aidan. Maybe even a little bit for Mel who had shown her nothing but kindness in the years that he'd lived in her home, in all the time she'd called him daddy.

It hurt to see the man she'd made love to with heart and soul last night draw a gun on her mother and her long-ago father.

The hurt grew into full-fledged panic when Mel finally noticed Aidan and shoved her mother away with both hands. Brianne's feet moved without her conscious permission, running out the French doors toward the scene on the lawn. Toward her fallen mother.

She saw Mel duck into the thick planting of hibiscus

bushes that towered at least eight feet tall. Saw Aidan shout a warning to his adversary although her heart pounded too hard to discern the words as she reached her mother and knelt by her side.

She heard the gunshot all too clearly.

The sharp crack split the air, sending Pauline into Brianne's arms and Melvin out of the hibiscus hedge, hands raised in surrender.

Unharmed.

Thank God.

Brianne hadn't realized she'd been holding her breath until it all whooshed out her lungs in a rush. She collapsed against her mother who already clung to her for all she was worth. Pauline's tears bathed her arms while they watched Aidan handcuff Mel and talk to him in a voice too low for them to hear.

"He caught me off guard," Pauline whispered through tears. "I didn't want him here. And I told him I couldn't go to the bank with him like he asked. Then he kissed me." Cheeks flushed, she blinked up at Brianne. Her neat twist at the back of her head had come unwound. "I shouldn't have let him kiss me, but I thought he just wanted to say goodbye."

Knowing Melvin, Brianne had the feeling the kiss stemmed from a desire to cajole more than any honorable notion of walking away. But she murmured only comforting words to her mother, not wishing to upset her further.

Brianne looked around the backyard as neighbors emerged from their houses. Dogs barked. A siren wailed in the distance.

Chaos in Palm Beach. Definitely not the kind of public attention Pauline would have ever wanted.

Realizing her mother needed her now more than ever, she lifted them both to their feet and wished like hell she had a remote that could rewind the whole day and set everything back to rights. For herself as well. Today's scene served as a too-potent reminder of how much the Wolcott women sucked at relationships.

Watching Aidan in motion before her very eyes bore little resemblance to the suspenseful action she had occasionally dramatized in her work as a filmmaker.

This sort of drama left her a bit shell-shocked. Speechless. She'd been through so many emotions in the last twenty-four hours she didn't know what to feel any more.

As police sirens neared the house and whined to a stop out front, Aidan took calls on his cell phone and spoke to the swarm of officers who appeared on the scene.

Brianne settled her mother in the house with migraine medicine and a good book, then returned to the lawn to clean up a couple of potted plants that had been knocked over during the incident.

By then, Aidan had sent Melvin off with someone. And although Brianne hadn't necessarily wanted to renew her relationship with a criminal, it still felt odd that she hadn't even said so much as hello or goodbye to the man who'd saved her from caviar and toast points in her lunch box.

Now, Aidan made his way over to her, stooping to help her as she righted a pot of jasmine cuttings that had only just started to take root.

''Are you okay?'' He brushed spilled dirt back into the terra-cotta pot, his voice conveying a hint of tender concern. Or had that been wishful thinking on her part?

Brianne didn't trust her scrambled senses to decide. Clearing her throat, she managed to nod. Speak. ''I'm fine. Shaken, but fine.''

He gestured toward the throng of blue uniforms on the lawn and the two guys in suits and shades that Brianne suspected were FBI associates. ''I've got about ten places I need to be this afternoon, but first I wanted to make sure you were all right.''

The words permeated some of the residual numbness still clinging to her. He needed to leave. Wanted her blessing on his way out the door. Gun in hand.

She wiped excess dirt off the jasmine leaves and nodded, unable to meet those intense gray eyes of his. ''I'm going to stick around here for a little while until my mother is settled. I need to talk to her anyway.''

She'd come to Pauline's house for a conversation this afternoon and in light of the gunshot and the arrest on the lawn, the topic had never been more timely. Her mother needed to swear off dangerous men.

As for Brianne, she needed to figure out if she could handle Aidan's hazardous crusade to keep South Beach safe, especially now that she understood how much that mission required him to put himself at risk.

Her brush with the reality of Aidan's day-to-day life left her chilled, uncertain.

''I'm sorry about this morning.'' Aidan tugged the terra-cotta pot out of her hand and set the plant aside. He peered over his shoulder at the mass of cops and federal agents as they fended off a growing crowd of reporters on the lawn. "It's just that I had a lot on my mind with the investigation and I know you don't want to get drawn into that. For that matter, I'm pretty sure you're uncomfortable about my job altogether."

He studied her as if waiting for her to deny it.

And she wanted to. But how could she pretend she wasn't scared of something happening to him when he hunted down members of the Most Wanted list for a living? She wasn't naive enough to think all of his prey would be white-collar criminals who wore seersucker and brought teddy bears to lonely little girls.

"You're in a dangerous line of work, Aidan. I think it would intimidate a lot of people. And my life has been filled with too much upheaval to handle a relationship with no emotional security." She brushed the dirt off her fingers, rubbed a spot off her slim black dress and tried not to meet his gaze.

Their future that had seemed filled with possibility last night had grown far more frightening this morning.

Staring back at her flurry of movement, Aidan didn't need to use his investigative skills to figure out what Brianne was feeling right now. He caught her wrist and held it until she looked up at him.

The fear in her eyes, the hesitation in her voice said it all. She couldn't handle his lifestyle any more than Natalie ever had.

No matter that Natalie had looked the part of a fragile flower while Brianne had been a firecracker for ten years and counting. Just because Brianne had grown adept at hiding her vulnerability didn't make it any less real.

He told himself her withdrawal didn't hurt. That he

was okay with this. "Not a problem. I would never try to put you in a situation that would ultimately cause you grief. Been there, done that, signed the divorce papers to prove it."

The words sounded colder than he'd intended. But damn it, he was feeling pretty damn cold inside today.

"I didn't mean to suggest—"

"Can you look me in the eye and tell me you're not scared of this, Bri?"

She blinked twice, quickly. And from the mixture of confusion and disappointment in her gaze, he knew she didn't stand a chance of telling him otherwise.

An ache shot through him. Disappointment. Regret. He hadn't expected it to tug at him so strongly.

Maybe because she was a woman so well matched for him, even if she would never recognize it. Despite the fact that she preferred to live behind the safety of a few lenses and lots of security controls, she still possessed more strength and flat-out chutzpah than most men he knew.

How would it feel to have that kind of woman watching out for you?

She had nerves of steel when it came to most anything but his job.

He reached to touch her face. Marveled at the softness of her skin. Wished that touch didn't have to be the last. "Then you're off the hook, Brianne. Free and clear."

Shouts from the lawn competed for his attention. Pulled him back to his job.

"You'd better go." Her words tumbled out of her mouth in a rush as if she welcomed the opportunity to end their conversation. Welcomed the chance to say goodbye.

With a heart full of regret, he brushed a thumb over the fullness of her lips.

Already missing their taste.

15

SHORTLY PAST SUNSET, Brianne finally found the video she'd scoured her house for beside an overgrown cactus and underneath the basket of clothes to take to the cleaners. *Dangerous Men and the Women Who Love Them*—the documentary she'd filmed last year after flying around the country to talk to countless flirts and daredevils, heartbreakers and bad boys.

She only hoped she hadn't found the video too late.

Judging by the shaky feelings of leftover panic that had dogged her since the afternoon, Brianne feared she was already half in love with Aidan. She'd always approached her relationships with just a little detachment in the past, careful not to get caught up in emotions—or men—she couldn't handle.

Granted, she screwed up in that department on a regular basis—hence her run-in with the stalker boyfriend. But she'd tried to maintain reasonable defenses with guys in the past.

But Aidan had plowed past them with typical lack of concern for rules or boundaries, barging into her world on her security monitor screen and then heading straight for her heart in real life.

The telephone rang before she had the chance to do anything with her tape. She caught herself hurrying toward the receiver and stopped herself. Aidan had no reason to contact her after the way she'd called it quits this afternoon. And she didn't want to talk to anyone else. Summer had already called her twice since Melvin's arrest today, insisting she take the night off so Brianne wasn't concerned anybody would be calling from the club.

Lingering near the answering machine on the off chance that the call might be important—and not just because she secretly hoped to hear Aidan's voice on the tape—Brianne waited for her message to play. Hands pressed, white-knuckled to the cool, pristine tiles of her kitchen island, she listened for the beep.

Silence on the other end.

Not a dial tone. Not a hang-up.

Just silence.

Someone waiting for her to answer? Fear crawled up the back of her neck as it occurred to her that although Aidan had assured her Jimmy was in New York early yesterday morning, he hadn't discovered whether or not Jimmy knew her current whereabouts.

Her eyes darted to the shiny new set of kitchen knives by her espresso machine.

But then, the phone connection clicked and a dial tone kicked in for a split second before the answering machine rewound the message.

She'd need to start making a diary of the hang-ups for the police, just in case. The recent rash of calls could be coincidental, but she hadn't survived months of stalking in New York by writing off episodes like this as coincidence.

Willing her breathing back to normal, Brianne purposely returned her focus to Aidan and the video in her hand.

She fanned herself with the documentary tape as she moved back to the VCR. She really didn't *need* to watch it since she still recalled half the script and all the dangerous male archetypes anyhow. Jimmy Vanderwalk had been a brooding poet. Aidan tended more toward the daredevil category.

But damn it, there was more to Aidan than that and she knew it. She'd romanticized Jimmy's brooding into sensitivity and she'd paid for it dearly. That didn't mean she had to overcompensate for her mistake by reading into Aidan's risk-taking.

He didn't take risks for the sake of the thrill, after all. There was a nobility about his job that had attracted her ten years ago and continued to draw her now. After having tangled with enough men who walked on the wrong side of the law, Brianne found she appreciated Aidan's sense of honor.

Still, that didn't change the fact that his job scared her to her toenails.

Officially depressed, Brianne tossed the video documentary onto the shelf where it should have been in the first place. She stared down at the row of her favorite movie titles, the backlogs of unused film footage she'd shot on various assignments and the overflow of security video feeds taken at the club over the last two weeks.

Including the very steamy footage of her and Aidan tangling limbs in the harem-themed room at the resort.

Not that she'd checked out the tape or anything. She'd been tempted, but so far she had managed not to play voyeur on that particular scene. Somehow, it didn't seem fair to watch them kissing, touching, heating up the screen without him by her side. How would she feel if he ever watched a video like that without her?

Flattered.

Unsure whether or not she was simply giving herself justification for what she wanted to do all along, Brianne tugged the video off the shelf and cracked open the clear plastic case. Shoving the contraband into her VCR she picked up her new all-inclusive house remote from on top of the television and dimmed the lights with the touch of a button. Clicked play on the VCR with another.

She had no clue why she wanted to torture herself with images of her and Aidan when her heart already ached at the idea of losing him.

Now that his investigation had ended, there would be no more long nights sitting side by side in her office. No more encounters on her desk or in the harem. She would go back to being detached. Alone. But safe.

The tape whirred to life inside the machine. A noise just outside her window distracted her, made her grateful she had her house remote still in hand so she could double-check her security. The doors were locked. Windows bolted. Alarm activated.

Could she be any more paranoid? No woman who jumped at every bump in the night could weather a relationship with an FBI agent. A fact that sucked in so many ways Brianne couldn't begin to enumerate them, let alone decipher which one had made tears pool in her eyes.

Sniffling, sighing, she heaved herself on to the love-seat and settled in to watch the show. Maybe if she granted herself this one last look at Aidan, a few moments to indulge all her heart's hungry might-have-beens, she'd be able to walk away for good.

If only she could have this final peek, maybe she could find the courage to burn the tape and move on with her life.

Too bad the man on the screen in his suit jacket and crisp white shirt didn't look like the kind of guy a woman could walk away from.

She sat in the dark smiling past the tear sliding down her cheek as she watched Aidan on screen. The video had just reached the point where Brianne tumbled the wall of rattan baskets to get to him.

Her bittersweet enjoyment of the moment was marred only by her delusions that a noise sounded outside her window again.

Probably just neighborhood dogs.

Still, her heart pounded with an odd mix of lingering paranoia from the days when Jimmy had been stalking her and the definite turn-on factor of watching her on-screen self crawl on all fours to confront Aidan.

She'd looked like a woman on a mission.

Brianne held her breath in rapt fascination as she and Aidan loomed closer. But she experienced more than just the flare of heat from watching a kiss in the making. Her director's eye viewed the film from a more critical perspective, almost as if she was searching for the emotion behind an acting performance.

Body tense, she saw the on-screen couple hover near one another. Then move toward one another like magnets in slow motion, drawn together like forces of nature.

And in that moment of silver screen drama, Brianne saw what had eluded her in real life.

The woman melting into Aidan on her television set was in love. Wildly, madly and passionately in love.

She loved Aidan.

The news thudded down on her with the force of a director's slate snapping closed between takes. How could she have missed it when the truth stared back at her so obviously from the celluloid pictures flashing on the television in front of her? Her heart jumped, skipped, fluttered with the realization.

The scene on the screen exploded into an R-rated kiss, making Brianne's body ache to relive the moment, making her heart yearn to act on this newly discovered love.

As for Aidan being a dangerous guy—she wondered if that was just an excuse. Maybe half the reason she went for troublemakers of all kinds in the past had been a way of keeping a *real* relationship at arm's length.

Falling for dangerous men had always kept her heart safe. Until now.

Although, as she watched the enraptured couple kissing on the screen, Brianne realized that all this time she'd probably been running from Aidan and not his job.

Behind her, another noise outside caught her attention. The sound made her jump, and for a split second she wondered if Aidan might be dropping by to talk to her tonight after all.

Until her bay window overlooking the back yard shattered.

Jimmy Vanderwalk plowed his way through the breach, stumbling and falling in a sea of jagged glass.

Brianne tried to scream, but her voice failed her. Which was just as well since she probably only had about five more seconds to save herself before he recovered.

Clutching the house remote in her hand, she reached for the cordless phone still at her side and pressed the number three button on speed dial.

Aidan.

She lifted the receiver to her ear with painful slowness, not wanting to alert her intruder to her intent too soon.

Still, she could hear the phone ringing.

And ringing.

Please let him be there.

Jimmy started to move. Glass shifted and fell to the floor from the folds of his clothes as he rose to his feet. A cut on his forehead spilled blood down his cheek while his smaller scratches covered his arms. He wore jeans with a rumpled concert T-shirt bearing the name of an up-and-coming rock band.

Cradled a sleek black gun in his right hand.

"Hello?" Aidan's voice in the telephone receiver sounded so far away.

As Jimmy's eyes focused, his gaze landed on the phone in Brianne's hand.

Words tumbled out of her mouth in a rush. "Help me, Aidan—"

A shot blasted through her house, cutting her off.

For an instant she thought *she'd* been hit until she realized she could hear the dead air where the phone had been shot off the wall.

"And just what the hell do you think you're doing?" Jimmy held the gun in a white-knuckled grip as he stalked closer.

"Nothing." She choked out the word, afraid he'd shoot her, too.

Panic welled with his every approaching step. How could her ex-boyfriend be here in her living room among shards of broken glass when Aidan had just spoken to him in New York less than two days ago?

Brianne shook off enough of her trancelike fear to scuttle backward off the couch, all the while keeping her eye on him.

His eye roved to the television where Aidan was slowly undressing her. The gun, however, remained pointed in her direction.

"I swear to God I would have knocked on the door if I hadn't seen this shit through the window." He swung the gun around to gesture toward the television screen, but his eyes looked too wild, too on the edge for Brianne to use the moment to run. "What the hell am I going to do with you, Brianne? Of all the faithless…"

His words spiraled downward into a gutter-spew of vulgarities Brianne refused to hear.

Answering him with fear-induced silence she scavenged to find her voice. Had Aidan heard her plea before their call disconnected? Had he recognized her voice on the other end?

She'd give anything for a dangerous guy like Aidan

to arrive and kick some serious ass right about now. Of course, suddenly Aidan's dangerous tendency struck her as more akin to a guardian angel's than a daredevil's. Why hadn't she ever tried to see that big-picture reality before? Her heart slammed so viciously against her chest she felt pummeled from the inside out, her body rebelling against her and the situation in which she found herself.

Then Jimmy shot the television.

Glass exploded out from the screen. Blue sparks jumped from the wasted machinery while the steaming shell of lacquer cabinetry echoed with popping and hissing sounds.

Holy crap.

"Answer me, damn you!" He shouted the words, crunching through the glass-covered carpet to loom over her. "What the hell were you doing kissing another guy?"

Shaking with fear and the realization that Jimmy had gone off the deep end somewhere between here and New York, Brianne dug her nails into the cold hard plastic in her hand. The house remote.

She squeezed the new gadgetry in her hand, an idea taking shape. To buy time she blurted out the first answer that came to mind. "It was a mistake. A movie I was making. The kiss you saw on the screen wasn't real."

"Don't tell me your cold-as-frigging-ice lies." His breath reeked of sickness. Madness, for all she knew. "I warned you not to mess around on me."

Her eyes fell on the gun despite her best efforts to look at him. She forced words out of her mouth to keep him distracted, to give him something to think about besides killing her then and there. "I was going to call you about the movie, actually. I thought you might put together a soundtrack for me."

There wasn't a chance in hell Aidan would show up now to play guardian angel for her. Thanks to her inability to see beyond the filter of her bad experiences with the men in her past, she'd called it quits with him when she should have been working harder to understand him.

But even if she didn't have his solid presence to rely on, she still had his wisdom. And Aidan had shown her how to think outside the box.

Brianne didn't need a gun to defend herself. Sometimes it worked to pretend to be a telemarketer. Well, not in this case. But she could definitely call upon her own strengths in this situation as opposed to running away from a gun she couldn't fight.

She wouldn't play in Jimmy's court. She'd lead him into hers.

Sure, she'd never fought off a criminal before, but she'd choreographed plenty of fight scenes for her films. And she knew a thing or two about utilizing special effects.

"Damn you and your lies." He stared at her across the living room with glazed eyes. Stalked after her into the hallway.

With unkempt hair and a face full of scruff that hadn't seen a razor in weeks, Jimmy looked nothing like the man she'd dated. As he closed the distance between them she smelled alcohol—possibly days' worth of alcohol judging by his wrinkled clothes and the sharp acidity of his scent.

"You're a long way from home." She commented only to buy herself time as she walked backward, hoping she could get him where she wanted him.

Praying he wouldn't shoot her first. She wanted the chance to tell Aidan she finally understood he wasn't such a dangerous guy after all. That his quick thinking had inspired her plan to get out of this mess.

"No shit, Sherlock." Jimmy peered around her house with his red-rimmed gaze. "I wouldn't be here if you hadn't skipped town without even telling me. Now, I come all this way and it turns out you're screwing around on me behind my back. I'm not a happy man, Brianne."

The back of her calf hit the bench in her foyer. The same bench she'd been sitting on the day Aidan had shown up at her house unexpectedly and caught her staring at erotic statues. She should have made love with him on the floor like she'd wanted to. Instead she'd walked away because of her fears. And now she might never have the chance to roll around with Aidan on the foyer floor.

Her eyes itched with unshed tears while her heart ached with regret.

"Don't even think about heading out that door, Brianne." Jimmy's angry tone sliced through her thoughts, called her back to the present with frightening clarity. "I've got at least three bullets in here with your name on them if you get any closer to the exit."

His threat cemented her resolve, stiffened her spine. She couldn't pretend that maybe he only wanted to talk to her or that maybe this encounter could end peacefully. He'd broken into her house with a gun and he intended to use it.

Her fingers flexed around the master remote she still clutched in her right hand. She couldn't afford to give away her plan with her eyes, but she sensed she'd drawn Jimmy into the proper position.

Aidan told her once she was hell on wheels, and there was no time like the present to prove him right. She hoped.

"I'm not going anywhere." She felt for the circular button on the bottom right of her remote and squeezed it as she talked in an effort to mask the ensuing noise. "But you might be."

He didn't look up until the last second.

And he was either too drunk or too surprised to move.

Brianne's massive hallway chandelier rushed down toward the floor in response to her flick of the switch. Thankfully, she hadn't had a chance to fix her faulty wiring job that had the contraption moving at high speed.

The heavy wrought-iron fixture clanged him in the head and brought him to the floor, effectively imprisoning him between the bars.

Not that he needed to be imprisoned. He slumped on the floor in what looked to be a total knockout.

Brianne scrambled for the gun, unwilling to rely on her visual assessment of his condition. In the films she made, the bad guy never went down the first time. Picking up the heavy steel, she tested the weight of the weapon and turned it on him. Just in case.

She hadn't fought this much of the battle only to have him shoot her while her back was turned.

After having been stalked, followed, harassed, vandalized and held at gunpoint tonight, she planned to live long enough to tell Aidan she wasn't afraid of his job, her feelings or taking a few chances anymore.

AIDAN'S BRAKES SQUEALED as he steered his flying car into Brianne's driveway, taking out half a row of hedges.

Fear twisted his insides, had been riding in his throat the whole way across town from the Palm Beach police headquarters. Thank God he'd been there and not down at his office in Miami when Brianne's call came.

Help me.

He vaulted what was left of the hedges in his haste to get to Brianne, praying he wouldn't be too late. He could have sworn the sound that cut them off had been a gunshot. His feet pounded across the lawn, the leaden weight of his shoes sprinting over the grass at only half the tempo of his racing heart.

He'd been in the middle of wading through mountains of paperwork, talking to the press and initiating a high-level investigation into Jackson Taggart's father when the call came that knocked him off his foundations.

Scared the hell out of him.

The cops were minutes behind him, but he wouldn't wait. Couldn't wait.

Those three frightening words from Brianne—*help me, Aidan*—had brought everything that was important to him into immediate, razor-sharp focus.

He'd been running scared from the connection between them this morning and now he'd trade anything to have it back. To be given another chance with Bri.

As he reached the front door, he turned the knob. Nothing.

A soft cry emanated from somewhere inside the house. Terrified of what might be happening to her, Aidan shot the lock and blasted his way through the door.

He didn't have to look far to find her. She sat slumped on the stairs at the end of the foyer in a house that looked like a war zone. Rubble covered the floor. Tears stained her cheeks.

"Aidan." Her voice whispered hoarsely across the distance that separated them.

He plowed his way through the glass and debris to get to her as a mixture of relief and rage flooded him, welcome emotions in the aftermath of the chilling fear that had held him in a vise grip ever since her phone call. Relief she was all right. Rage at what she must have been through.

She held a gun in one hand now.

Trained on a body lying on her hallway floor.

Aidan's years in the FBI helped him put together the crime scene faster than she could have ever explained it to him. The broken window, the glass everywhere.

Reaching her side he slid his arms around her and slipped the gun from her hand. He held her for precious seconds, absorbing the warmth, the incredible strength of her slender body in his hands.

His eyes burned. His head pounded at the thought of what could have happened to her.

And the love he felt for her couldn't have been more obvious.

"I was so damn scared." He swiped a thumb across her cheek, drying her tears. "Are you okay?"

She nodded against his shoulder and some of his rage subsided as relief overwhelmed him.

Still, he couldn't deny a twinge of grim happiness when he saw the body on the floor twitch.

He set Brianne aside, his fingers already clenching as her attacker shook his head as if to clear his vision. At least Aidan hoped that's what happened. Because he wanted to make certain the guy got a damn good look at the fist careening toward his face.

Violence had never felt so fulfilling.

Reassured that the guy was down for the count until the local police arrived, Aidan turned back to Brianne. Gut still churning with residual fear, he scrubbed a hand across his face and met her gaze. "Call me a dangerous guy all you want, but I'm not apologizing for wanting to kill him."

"He would have killed me." Her green eyes conveyed new understanding, a quiet acceptance of Aidan's words. "But the police can handle the punishment. You and I have done more than our share to fight him off. It's not up to us anymore."

The wail of the sirens already grew in the distance and Aidan knew they didn't have time left to talk. They'd be stuck answering questions for hours.

So he used the remaining moments to pull her in his arms and feel the jumpy beat of her heart. Listen to her breath whoosh in and out past his ear as he squeezed her to him.

He didn't know how the police would be able to question her because he didn't think he'd ever be able to let her go.

16

"I STILL CAN'T BELIEVE you knocked him out with the chandelier." Aidan shook his head as he heaved Brianne's suitcase onto the luggage stand in Honeymoon Heaven on the top floor of Club Paradise. He slumped against the windowsill and turned back to her with that same disbelieving expression he'd worn for the last two hours.

They'd answered all the questions the police had for them and Aidan had spoken to several officers privately to suggest increased protection for Brianne on the off chance Jimmy was released on bail before his trial. Brianne had the feeling her house would be thoroughly patrolled for the rest of her life.

Now, she planned to sleep at the club in one of the old rooms until her home could be cleaned and the window repaired. She clutched the coffee cup Aidan had filled for her on their way out of the police station and smiled up at him.

Warmth spiraled through her, and not just because of the potent brew. Aidan had repeated this same phrase at least ten times since appearing at her door to discover her with an unconscious criminal imprisoned on her foyer floor. He couldn't believe she'd brought down a gun-wielding assailant with a chandelier.

"I can't believe he made it all the way from New York to Palm Beach without us knowing about it." Brianne remembered Aidan had flagged Jimmy's credit card accounts so they'd know if he bought gas out of state. He'd also found a way to be alerted if her psycho ex-boyfriend purchased plane tickets. So why hadn't they known he was on his way to Florida ahead of time?

"When I went to grab the coffee one of the detectives told me Vanderwalk hitched a ride on a tour bus with a band. He probably left New York a few hours after I called him the other day." He pounded the windowsill in an absent rhythm with his fist. "I'm so sorry he got by me, Brianne."

Abandoning her coffee cup to the dresser full of gilded cherub statues and heart-shaped mirrors, she crossed the carpet. Closed the distance between them to face the man she'd longed for in the scariest moments of her life.

"You don't have anything to be sorry for. Nothing." She pulled a crisp new baseball cap out of his hands— a token bestowed upon him during his meeting with the Palm Beach police chief—and set it on the nightstand behind her. "You couldn't have possibly known he would be at my house tonight."

"But in the course of one day you had to see *me* pull a gun on Melvin, and then *you* had to stare down the nose of a pistol. If you were opposed to the violence in my job before, I can't begin to imagine how you're going to feel about it now." He brushed his hands up her arms, ran his fingers back down through her hair. "I can't leave my job yet because I just started overseeing a new investigation of the guy who sabotaged my case against Mel the first time around. After that, if you want me to walk away from it, I will.''

Brianne knew that kind of sacrifice would probably be akin to someone throwing away all his baseball caps *and* his mirrored sunglasses. Still, the words didn't even stick in his throat.

''And just what would you do if you weren't a kick-ass FBI agent, Maddock? Somehow I can't envision you getting into telemarketing on a full-time basis.'' Although she could see him being successful at most anything despite his unconventional approach to life.

''Maybe I'd talk you into showing me a little gadgetry. I bet there's a future in high-speed chandelier lowering devices. You may have come up with the next wave in home security.'' He reached for the ball cap she'd put on the table and shook the crisp newness out of it before settling it on his head. Palm Beach Police was stitched across the front in yellow letters along with a series of small stars.

''I would never want you to leave the FBI.'' Still, she loved him for suggesting it. Loved him for being willing to follow through with it. ''You're too good at what you do to give it up for me.''

''You're missing my point. I want to be with you, Brianne, and I'm willing to do whatever it takes to make that happen. You can't sidestep that by telling me I *can't* give up the FBI. I *want* to give it up.'' His hands roamed down to her waist and paused on her hips. ''I want you.''

The heat of his touch permeated the thin fabric of

her dress, warmed her skin despite the chill that had been dogging her all night. "I'm not the one missing the point here, Maddock. I want you, too. And that means I want the kick-ass crime buster, not another techno-geek to help me with my gadgets. I'm not about to let you leave the Bureau."

"Kick-ass crime busting?" His hands slid away from her, his fingers flexing into clenched fists at his side. He pounded the tacky gilded dresser so hard all the cupid figurines jumped. "Thanks to my total lack of kick-ass ability you nearly died tonight at the hands of a lunatic, Bri. Where was I when you needed me? How the hell can you say I'd be better off at the FBI?" He squeezed his palm across his forehead, his fingers and thumbs practically biting into his temples as he turned away from her toward the door. "I'll go check the security monitors downstairs and make sure things are running smoothly in the club while you get settled."

Apparently he didn't realize they were officially through walking away from one another. Brianne reached for his shoulder and tugged, effectively halting him in his tracks.

"You think you weren't there tonight, Aidan? Do you really think *I* kicked ass all by myself? *Me*, who is so afraid of real life that I lock myself in my office and watch it all from behind a camera lens or a computer monitor?" She slugged him—gently—on one broad shoulder. "If it hadn't been for you, *I* probably would have gotten shot instead of my television. If left to my own devices, I would have just cowered behind the sofa because I was so scared I couldn't scream and I couldn't move. You know what saved me?"

He didn't ask, but his eyebrows lifted just a little.

"*You* did. You and your brilliantly ridiculous idea of pretending to be a telemarketer when you called New York the other day." She gulped past the lump in her throat that had been growing ever since Aidan had moved toward the door. "I told myself that if you could crack cases by pretending to be a telemarketer, then I ought to be able to fight crime by calling on my own strengths."

"Your gadgets." The stern lines of his face relaxed. Softened.

"Exactly."

He closed his eyes. Shook his head. And smiled. "Woman, I am so damn in love with you it hurts."

"Really?" Brianne felt like a goofy eighteen-year-old again, staring up at the hunky federal agent with stars in her eyes.

"Honest and damn truly." He cradled her face in his hands, stroked her cheek with the pad of one callused thumb. "I'm trying to respect your space, I'm trying not to crowd you after you've been traumatized, I'm trying to cope with the fact that I screwed up and let a murderous SOB get past me, but all I really want to do is beg you to come home with me and never leave."

Happiness bloomed inside her on the most unlikely day of her life. She'd woken up to a crumpled note instead of a lover, she'd weathered two arrests and survived a showdown at gunpoint. Yet she had the feeling she would remember today as one of the best in her whole life. ''Then let's forget about my space because I've decided I don't want it anymore. In fact, I want as little as possible.''

Aidan obliged so fast her head was still spinning when his lips settled over hers. He kissed her with hunger and longing, his hands pressing her whole body to his in head-to-toe connection.

''You may never have any space again,'' he whispered, backing her toward the bed.

But Brianne halted, not ready to lose herself in a sensual firestorm just yet. She had something important to say. Pulling back from Aidan's kiss, she put her hands on his chest for a very temporary barrier.

''I love you, too.'' She blurted the words with zero finesse and all feeling. ''I meant to tell you before but I got distracted by the kiss.''

''Even with the job?'' His brow furrowed, obviously not understanding what she was telling him.

''You *are* the job, Aidan. And I want you exactly the way I found you.'' The time had come for her to put a little of his dangerous muscle on her side—someone to fight with her and for her when times got tough.

He grinned that purely male smile that made her insides tingle. ''Then I'm definitely taking you home. We can spend tonight in Honeymoon Heaven and tomorrow night in pure bliss at my place.'' He backed her closer to the bed and gently tackled her to the mattress.

She laughed, amazed how much joy she could squeeze out of a hideous day. ''You really mean it about me coming home with you?''

''Hell yes. You can't go back to your house until

the glass is fixed. And maybe not even then. I don't think we're going to be able to do this with you living in Palm Beach and me in South Beach.'' His gray eyes roamed over her as if searching for answers to questions he hadn't asked yet. ''I have the feeling we'll figure something out.''

She stared up at him, trailed her fingers up the strong arms that bracketed her as he held himself above her and shared the thought that had been chasing around the back of her mind. ''I already have one part figured out.''

He rolled to one side of her and slid a hand down to her hip and then spanned the breadth of her belly with one heated palm. ''I have one part of this figured out, too.''

''Not that.'' Heat curled through her at his touch. ''I just wanted you to know I've already got a plan for helping you make your job less dangerous.''

''You're going to keep me tied to the bed pleasuring you night and day?''

She had to smile at the hopeful look in his eyes. ''Actually, I thought I'd work on those techno-gadgets you mentioned. I'm sure if I put my mind to it I can come up with a few projects to help you do your job better. More safely.''

''And what could you possibly do as a follow-up act to the swinging chandelier? How about some spy cameras or dart-shooting pencils? I really think you've got a future in gadgets. You can be Q to my James Bond, only a hell of a lot better looking.''

Brianne rolled her eyes as Aidan unbuttoned her dress with slow precision. ''First I'm making a documentary about stalkers I think. Maybe I'll be able to help other women if I do a little behind-the-camera investigation of my own.''

Pausing in his work on the buttons, he kissed her head. "Smart woman. But I really think the crime busters of the world would jump all over the dart-shooting pencils.''

"Fine, dart-shooting pencils it is.'' She reached for the nightstand to dim the lamp then twined her arms around his neck. "But first, I need to make sure you're safe from female predators when you're out in the field. Maybe something along the lines of exploding lighters for you to offer those pushy cigarette girls.''

Aidan's lips brushed hers, his fingers picking up speed on the buttons of her dress now. "You're still a firecracker, Brianne.''

She stole the baseball cap from his head and plunked it on hers.

"I just believe in taking some basic security measures.'' She shivered as he slid away the two halves of her dress, allowing the air to brush over her exposed skin.

"Then you're going to love the present I have in mind for you.'' He unwound her fingers from his hair and laid a single kiss in her palm. "It's a little sign you wear on your left hand and it tells the rest of the world to back off—this woman's taken....''

You haven't seen the last of
SINGLE IN SOUTH BEACH!

Joanne Rock's series returns with
Jackson and Summer's story in

GIRL'S GUIDE TO HUNTING & KISSING

Harlequin Blaze 108

Coming in October 2003

Turn the page for a sneak preview....

1

SUMMER FARNSWORTH was doing her best to fend him off, damn it, and Jackson wanted no part of it.

She swayed toward him slightly, her eyelids fluttering but refusing to fall.

"I'm the kind of person who craves freedom. I break rules all the time. Just for fun." Her voice held a note of warning, mild panic. "Didn't I tell you I was the original bad girl behind the Bad-Girl Bordello?"

Jackson Taggart had no interest in being warned off. The temperature between them cranked up a few more degrees, giving him no choice but to pull her to him and mold her slender body to his.

"I don't see you breaking any rules tonight, Summer. If I'm going to be convinced you're such a bad girl, I think you're going to have to prove it."

Proof?

Summer blinked and tried to clear her mind of the sensual fog surrounding her. She had greeted the man with her bustier untied and now she was practically unraveling in his arms from just a touch, yet he required *proof* of her wild and wanton streak?

Well by God, she would gladly show him.

Stretching up on her toes, she brushed her lips over his the way she'd wanted to for the last hour. Sitting beside the sexy attorney in the lush sensuality of the bordello room had made her more than a little edgy. And since the kiss was simply an exercise in proving a point, she didn't bother to hold anything back.

She flicked her tongue across his lips to steal a taste. He possessed a full, soft mouth for a man of such chiseled features and hard angles. Her eyelids fell shut, heightening the sensations of his kiss. The warm whiskey taste of him intoxicated her, made her even bolder.

Splaying a hand across his broad chest beneath his jacket, she absorbed the feel of starched cotton and warm muscle through his white dress shirt. Her fingertips itched to cover more ground, to explore the terrain of the rock-hard abs currently plastered against her. To follow the silky path of his tie to the leather of his belt and then dip lower still…

Yet she contented herself with reaching to touch his face, to cradle his rough-hewn jaw and stroke the crisp hair at the back of his neck. His aftershave smelled clean and expensive, elusive enough to make her want to linger so she might catch the scent more strongly.

But then Jackson expelled a throaty growl of pure male hunger and tightened his grip. Arms banded around her, he locked her body against his, his formerly still hands now coming to life.

He deepened their kiss, delving into her mouth to mate and join them. Summer closed her eyes more tightly against the onslaught of heat, the tingly wave of needy sensation that tripped through her whole body. As his tongue probed hers, an answering shock wave pulsed between her legs.

In the recesses of her brain, she heard the bluesy piano of Duke Ellington somewhere in the background, but even the vivid reds of the bordello were fading to black when forced to compete with the magnetic draw of this man.

Jackson.

The silk moire bustier that she'd retied now strained at the seams with her erratic breathing. She could already anticipate what it would feel like to peel off the stiff fabric and press herself intimately to Jackson's hard chest.

How had she ever thought Jackson was low-key or laid-back when he kissed with the exquisite finesse of the devil himself?

He backed her closer to the bed recessed in a private alcove of the larger room. Or perhaps she drew him toward the bed. It seemed their chemistry had exploded all of a sudden, leaving them both in the grip of a power that was hotter and more volatile then either of them.

Her thigh skimmed the red satin coverlet as the black lace grazed her ankle. The dull thud at the back of her leg barely fazed her, but it seemed to bring Jackson back to life.

He broke off their kiss, his eyes refocusing on their surroundings.

On her.

"That's not so bad in my book, Summer." His voice hit a smoky note, blending in with the gravelly blues singer emanating from the bedside radio.

"Damn straight it wasn't so bad," she whispered back, debating how difficult it would be to topple him down on to the bed with her. "In fact, that was down-right fantastic."

The distinct sound of a smothered laugh drew her attention from the logistics of maneuvering a six-foot-plus man into bed. Her gaze landed on a mouth suppressing a smile.

"I meant that *you* aren't so bad, Summer. As in, maybe you're not quite the bad girl you think you are."

Is your man too good to be true?

Hot, gorgeous AND romantic?
If so, he could be a Harlequin® Blaze™ series cover model!

Our grand-prize winners will receive a trip for two to New York City to
shoot the cover of a Blaze novel, and will stay at the luxurious Plaza Hotel.
Plus, they'll receive $500 U.S. spending money!
The runner-up winners will receive $200 U.S.
to spend on a romantic dinner for two.

It's easy to enter!

In 100 words or less, tell us what makes your boyfriend or spouse a true romantic
and the perfect candidate for the cover of a Blaze novel, and include in your submission
two photos of this potential cover model.

All entries must include the written submission of the contest entrant, two photographs of the model
candidate and the Official Entry Form and Publicity Release forms completed in full and signed by
both the model candidate and the contest entrant. Harlequin, along with the experts at
Elite Model Management, will select a winner.

For photo and complete Contest details, please refer to the Official Rules on the next page. All entries
will become the property of Harlequin Enterprises Ltd. and are not returnable.

**Please visit www.blazecovermodel.com to download a copy of the Official Entry Form and
Publicity Release Form or send a request to one of the addresses below.**

Please mail your entry to: **Harlequin Blaze Cover Model Search**

In U.S.A.	In Canada
P.O. Box 9069	P.O. Box 637
Buffalo, NY	Fort Erie, ON
14269-9069	L2A 5X3

No purchase necessary. Contest open to Canadian and U.S. residents who are 18 and over.
Void where prohibited. Contest closes September 30, 2003.

HARLEQUIN BLAZE COVER MODEL SEARCH CONTEST 3569 OFFICIAL RULES
NO PURCHASE NECESSARY TO ENTER

1. To enter, submit two (2) 4" x 6" photographs of a boyfriend or spouse (who must be 18 years of age or older) taken no later than three (3) months from the time of entry: a close-up, waist up, shirtless photograph; and a fully clothed, full-length photograph, then, tell us, in 100 words or fewer, why he should be a Harlequin Blaze cover model and how he is romantic. Your complete "entry" must include: (i) your essay, (ii) the Official Entry Form and Publicity Release Form printed below completed and signed by you (as "Entrant"), (iii) the photographs (with your hand-written name, address and phone number, and your model's name, address and phone number on the back of each photograph), and (iv) the Publicity Release Form and Photograph Representation Form printed below completed and signed by your model (as "Model"), and should be sent via first-class mail to either: Harlequin Blaze Cover Model Search Contest 3569, P.O. Box 9069, Buffalo, NY, 14269-9069, or Harlequin Blaze Cover Model Search Contest 3569, P.O. Box 637, Fort Erie, Ontario L2A 5X3. All submissions must be in English and be received no later than September 30, 2003. Limit: one entry per person, household or organization. **Purchase or acceptance of a product offer does not improve your chances of winning.** All entry requirements must be strictly adhered to for eligibility and to ensure fairness among entries.

2. Ten (10) Finalist submissions (photographs and essays) will be selected by a panel of judges consisting of members of the Harlequin editorial, marketing and public relations staff, as well as a representative from Elite Model Management (Toronto) Inc., based on the following criteria:

Aptness/Appropriateness of submitted photographs for a Harlequin Blaze cover—70%

Originality of Essay—20%

Sincerity of Essay—10%

In the event of a tie, duplicate finalists will be selected. The photographs submitted by finalists will be posted on the Harlequin website no later than November 15, 2003 (at www.blazecovermodel.com), and viewers may vote, in rank order, on their favorite(s) to assist in the panel of judges' final determination of the Grand Prize and Runner-up winning entries based on the above judging criteria. All decisions of the judges are final.

3. All entries become the property of Harlequin Enterprises Ltd. and none will be returned. Any entry may be used for future promotional purposes. Elite Model Management (Toronto) Inc. and/or its partners, subsidiaries and affiliates operating as "Elite Model Management" will have access to all entries including all personal information, and may contact any Entrant and/or Model in its sole discretion for their own business purposes. Harlequin and Elite Model Management (Toronto) Inc. are separate entities with no legal association or partnership whatsoever having no power to bind or obligate the other or create any expressed or implied obligation or responsibility on behalf of the other, such that Harlequin shall not be responsible in any way for any acts or omissions of Elite Model Management (Toronto) Inc. or its partners, subsidiaries and affiliates in connection with the Contest or otherwise and Elite Model Management shall not be responsible in any way for any acts or omissions of Harlequin or its partners, subsidiaries and affiliates in connection with the contest or otherwise.

4. All Entrants and Models must be residents of the U.S. or Canada, be 18 years of age or older, and have no prior criminal convictions. The contest is not open to any Model that is a professional model and/or actor in any capacity at the time of the entry. Contest void wherever prohibited by law; all applicable laws and regulations apply. Any litigation within the Province of Quebec regarding the conduct or organization of a publicity contest may be submitted to the Régie des alcools, des courses et des jeux for a ruling, and any litigation regarding the awarding of a prize may be submitted to the Régie only for the purpose of helping the parties reach a settlement. Employees and immediate family members of Harlequin Enterprises Ltd., D.L. Blair, Inc., Elite Model Management (Toronto) Inc. and their parents, affiliates, subsidiaries and all other agencies, entities and persons connected with the use, marketing or conduct of this Contest are not eligible to enter. Acceptance of any prize offered constitutes permission to use Entrants' and Models' names, essay submissions, photographs or other likenesses for the purposes of advertising, trade, publication and promotion on behalf of Harlequin Enterprises Ltd., its parent, affiliates, subsidiaries, assigns and other authorized entities involved in the judging and promotion of the contest without further compensation to any Entrant or Model, unless prohibited by law.

5. Finalists will be determined no later than October 30, 2003. Prize Winners will be determined no later than January 31, 2004. Grand Prize Winners (consisting of winning Entrant and Model) will be required to sign and return Affidavit of Eligibility/Release of Liability and Model Release forms within thirty (30) days of notification. Non-compliance with this requirement and within the specified time period will result in disqualification and an alternate will be selected. Any prize notification returned as undeliverable will result in the awarding of the prize to an alternate set of winners. All travelers (or parent/legal guardian of a minor) must execute the Affidavit of Eligibility/Release of Liability prior to ticketing and must possess required travel documents (e.g. valid photo ID) where applicable. Travel dates specified by Sponsor but no later than May 30, 2004.

6. Prizes: One (1) Grand Prize—the opportunity for the Model to appear on the cover of a paperback book from the Harlequin Blaze series, and a 3 day/2 night trip for two (Entrant and Model) to New York, NY for the photo shoot of Model which includes round-trip coach air transportation from the commercial airport nearest the winning Entrant's home to New York, NY, (or, in lieu of air transportation, $100 cash payable to Entrant and Model, if the winning Entrant's home is within 250 miles of New York, NY), hotel accommodations (double occupancy) at the Plaza Hotel and $500 cash spending money payable to Entrant and Model, (approximate prize value: $8,000), and one (1) Runner-up Prize of $200 cash payable to Entrant and Model for a romantic dinner for two (approximate prize value: $200). Prizes are valued in U.S. currency. Prizes consist of only those items listed as part of the prize. No substitution of prize(s) permitted by winners. All prizes are awarded jointly to the Entrant and Model of the winning entries, and are not severable - prizes and obligations may not be assigned or transferred. Any change to the Entrant and/or Model of the winning entries will result in disqualification and an alternate will be selected. Taxes on prize are the sole responsibility of winners. Any and all expenses and/or items not specifically described as part of the prize are the sole responsibility of winners. Harlequin Enterprises Ltd. and D.L. Blair, Inc., their parents, affiliates, and subsidiaries are not responsible for errors in printing of Contest entries and/or game pieces. No responsibility is assumed for lost, stolen, late, illegible, incomplete, inaccurate, non-delivered, postage due or misdirected mail or entries. In the event of printing or other errors which may result in unintended prize values or duplication of prizes, all affected game pieces or entries shall be null and void.

7. Winners will be notified by mail. For winners' list (available after March 31, 2004), send a self-addressed, stamped envelope to: Harlequin Blaze Cover Model Search Contest 3569 Winners, P.O. Box 4200, Blair, NE 68009-4200, or refer to the Harlequin website (at www.blazecovermodel.com).

Contest sponsored by Harlequin Enterprises Ltd., P.O. Box 9042, Buffalo, NY 14269-9042.

Your opinion is important to us! Please take a few moments to share your thoughts with us about your experiences with Harlequin and Silhouette books. Your comments will be very useful in ensuring that we deliver books you love to read. *Please take a few minutes to complete the questionnaire, then send it to us at the address below.*

Send your completed questionnaires to:
Harlequin/Silhouette Reader Survey, P.O. Box 9046, Buffalo, NY 14269-9046

1. As you may know, there are many different lines under the Harlequin and Silhouette brands. Each of the lines is listed below. Please check the box that most represents your reading habit for each line.

Line	Currently read this line	Do not read this line	Not sure if I read this line
Harlequin American Romance	❑	❑	❑
Harlequin Duets	❑	❑	❑
Harlequin Romance	❑	❑	❑
Harlequin Historicals	❑	❑	❑
Harlequin Superromance	❑	❑	❑
Harlequin Intrigue	❑	❑	❑
Harlequin Presents	❑	❑	❑
Harlequin Temptation	❑	❑	❑
Harlequin Blaze	❑	❑	❑
Silhouette Special Edition	❑	❑	❑
Silhouette Romance	❑	❑	❑
Silhouette Intimate Moments	❑	❑	❑
Silhouette Desire	❑	❑	❑

2. Which of the following best describes why you bought *this book*? One answer only, please.

the picture on the cover	❑	the title	❑
the author	❑	the line is one I read often	❑
part of a miniseries	❑	saw an ad in another book	❑
saw an ad in a magazine/newsletter	❑	a friend told me about it	❑
I borrowed/was given this book	❑	other: _____	❑

3. Where did you buy *this book*? One answer only, please.

at Barnes & Noble	❑	at a grocery store	❑
at Waldenbooks	❑	at a drugstore	❑
at Borders	❑	on eHarlequin.com Web site	❑
at another bookstore	❑	from another Web site	❑
at Wal-Mart	❑	Harlequin/Silhouette Reader	❑
at Target	❑	Service/through the mail	
at Kmart	❑	used books from anywhere	❑
at another department store or mass merchandiser	❑	I borrowed/was given this book	❑

4. On average, how many Harlequin and Silhouette books do you buy at one time?

I buy _____ books at one time ❑
I rarely buy a book ❑

MRQ403HB-1A

5. How many times per month do you shop for any *Harlequin and/or Silhouette* books? One answer only, please.

1 or more times a week	☐	a few times per year	☐
1 to 3 times per month	☐	less often than once a year	☐
1 to 2 times every 3 months	☐	never	☐

6. When you think of your ideal heroine, which *one* statement describes her the best? One answer only, please.

She's a woman who is strong-willed	☐	She's a desirable woman	☐
She's a woman who is needed by others	☐	She's a powerful woman	☐
She's a woman who is taken care of	☐	She's a passionate woman	☐
She's an adventurous woman	☐	She's a sensitive woman	☐

7. The following statements describe types or genres of books that you may be interested in reading. Pick *up to 2 types* of books that you are most interested in.

I like to read about truly romantic relationships	☐
I like to read stories that are sexy romances	☐
I like to read romantic comedies	☐
I like to read a romantic mystery/suspense	☐
I like to read about romantic adventures	☐
I like to read romance stories that involve family	☐
I like to read about a romance in times or places that I have never seen	☐
Other: _____	☐

The following questions help us to group your answers with those readers who are similar to you. Your answers will remain confidential.

8. Please record your year of birth below.

19 ____

9. What is your marital status?

single ☐   married ☐   common-law ☐   widowed ☐
divorced/separated ☐

10. Do you have children 18 years of age or younger currently living at home?

yes ☐   no ☐

11. Which of the following best describes your employment status?

employed full-time or part-time ☐   homemaker ☐   student ☐
retired ☐   unemployed ☐

12. Do you have access to the Internet from either home or work?

yes ☐   no ☐

13. Have you ever visited eHarlequin.com?

yes ☐   no ☐

14. What state do you live in?

_____

15. Are you a member of Harlequin/Silhouette Reader Service?

yes ☐   Account # _____   no ☐   MRQ403HB-1B

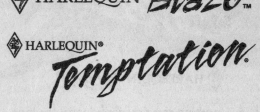

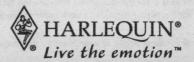

COMING NEXT MONTH

#105 NIGHT FEVER Tori Carrington
Kiss & Tell, Bk.1
Four friends. Countless secrets… Dr. Layla Hollister doesn't think she
has any secrets worth telling…until she throws caution to the winds and
indulges in an incredible one-night stand with a sexy stranger. A no-strings
encounter—exactly what the doctor ordered. That is, until Layla walks into
the clinic the next morning and discovers her mystery lover is really
her new boss. And he's expecting to pick up where they left off….

#106 PACKED WITH PLEASURE Lori Wilde
Gorgeous, confident Alec Ramsey—to fire up *her* engines?
Eden Montgomery's sure hoping so. He's exactly the adventure-hungry
daredevil she needs. Having lost her creative edge, she's counting on a
superhot tryst with Alec to not only inspire her sexy, one-of-a-kind gift
baskets, but her sexy, one-of-a-kind self!

#107 WICKED GAMES Alison Kent
www.girl-gear, Bk.2
gIRL-gEAR VP Kinsey Gray is not pleased to hear that Doug Storey
is moving away to Denver. She and the sexy architect have a history,
but Kinsey was never quite sure how she felt about him. Now that he's
leaving, it's time she made up her mind. With the help of a three-step plan
to seduce Doug, Kinsey's positive she'll persuade him to stick around. The
wicked games she has planned for him will knock *more* than his socks off!

#108 GIRL'S GUIDE TO HUNTING & KISSING Joanne Rock
Single in South Beach, Bk. 2
When Summer Farnsworth goes hunting for the perfect man to have a little
fling with, Jackson Taggart is not who she had in mind. There's not a rebel
bone—or a tattoo—under those too-starched shirts, or so she thinks. But
whoever said opposites attract must know something. Because after a few
long, steamy kisses, Summer has discovered a *big* attraction to the button-
down type.

Visit us at www.eHarlequin.com